Index of P

The Concerto 'o Boasters 12
Davie's Dairy Milk 16
A Game O' Cat An' Moose 17
Burke and Hare 18
It's Hard Being Eight 22
Jean Armour 26
The Loss of a Child 27
A Begging Letter to Nancy 28
The Aldi Blues 29
A Ferry Sets Sail 30
Culloden Field 16 April 1746 32
Glorified Tiddlywinks! 33
Bird Brain 34
A Passion For Poetry 35
Clootie Dumplin 36
A New Baby 38
Dave The Post Scot 40
Me and Billy 42
The Whisperin' Win' 44
Hush, Little One 45
The Tradesman 46
Summit Fever 49
Hunkert 50
Gordon Ramsay and Me 52
A Cannae Write a Poem 54
Memories of Mothers Day 55
An Ode Tae The Sun 56
Troglodyte 58
Losing Weight 59
A Great Nicht Wis Had By Aw 60
My Mistress Of Strategy 63
Childhood 64
The Patter of Tiny Feet 65
Jungle of Memories 66
Clones 69
Fighting Winter 70
72
73
74
No Harm See 79
Sad Craw 80
Second Time 83
Olympics London 2012 84
Roses Are Special 86
Holiday 87
Highland Games 88
My Only True Love 90
Farewell Mum 92
Flying Pyramids 94
My Colours 95
Weaver of Dreams 96
Granda's Wallies 97
On The Slopes O' Ben More 98
Our Dad 102
Ma Brither Jack 104
The Funeral 106
Trust You Ken 108
Hands Of A Craftsman 109
The Temptations of Food 110
The Courageous Fight 112
Tarzan in the Concrete Jungle 114
Memories Of Childhood 116
The Gardener 118
Three Generations 124
Wet Feet 126
The Tantrum Club 127
The Ship in a Boattle 128
Young and Old 130
Snowtime 133
William Tell 134
Jenny's Cruise 136
Wee TC 138

Quill Poetry and Writing Group

Quill Poetry Group was set up by myself, Lorna Johnston as a Millennium Project, in 2001, which was called 'Breaking Down Barriers'.

The aim was to bring the reading and writing of poetry into the community to fulfil the needs of all, no matter age or gender.

Funding from the Millennium was tantamount to making the project the success it has been. In the beginning we had big plans and I must say that we were a bit optimistic, as to how many would come along, but as time has progressed, we have seen many come and go over the 12 years since its creation.

As other groups have folded, Quill has continued

on its way and survived through a mixture of determination and courage.

Courage I say because we nearly did fold up a few years back when our secretary Donnie McNeill died suddenly. With lots of determination and a big pinch of luck we turned everything round and now we have a great group of different ages and strengths of characters to take us forward.

I have to pinch myself, when I see how good fortune has shone on the group I set up all those years ago and am grateful for the members who are with me in the group presently and know that it can only get better.

Here's to the next 12 years and more.

Paul Gallagher

Paul's introduction to writing came in the form of lyrics. At the early age of sweet sixteen he was singing in a punk band – that was the heady late seventies.

Writing music has stayed with Paul all the way through the noughties, fortunately – or unfortunately – not with the punk band. Playing, producing and singing original and creative music has always been his passion.

Whether it be writing about politics, love, science, themes historical or topical, everything is game. He is enormously influenced by the lyrical poetic rhymes of Dylan, Bowie, Lennon, not forgetting his grandfather, Patrick Lynch and of course ''Oh there was a little hen and it had a wooden leg ha ha''.

Always keen to improve his craft, Paul immersed himself in performance poetry and Quill Poetry group have enlightened and helped shape his signature story telling style.

"Always remember, never forget!"

May Ross

May Ross is 77 years of age and has always been interested in poetry, writing poems for her family, her church about things which she feels deserve to be put into rhyme.

May has one daughter and one granddaughter, who is the "love of my life."

Losing her husband in 2002 to cancer, May never remarried and remains very involved with her church and the West Lothian Highland Games.

Spending much loved time at her caravan in St. Fillans, she also enjoys knitting and sequence dancing, which "gets me out and keeps me fit."

Christine McGhie

Christine McGhie lives in Blackridge with her husband Matthew. They have been married for thirty five years. She owns and manages Mill House Cattery.

Writing was a childhood hobby and Christine recently started writing again when she joined Quill in the spring of 2013.

Other hobbies include a passion for singing, playing piano and guitar, putting her musical talents to organising and performing in Charity events.

She enjoys walking with her two Bearded Collies, Poppy and Bracken and lovingly caring for her three cats. She also enjoys Gardening.

"A poet once said that we are not born poets it is something within yourself that develops in your life and helps you to express yourself in words and verse."

Lorna Johnston

Lorna Johnston is the Treasurer of Quill Poetry Group. She is 59 years old and married with two children and one granddaughter. Poetry has been a mainstay all of her life. Something fulfilling and emotional.

Starting Quill Poetry Group in 2001 as a Millennium funded 'Breaking Down Barrier' project, Lorna has seen many come and go with different viewpoints and abilities in writing and reading poetry, but Quill has withstood the changes over the years retaining a good healthy vibrant group of "diehard poets of different strengths, capabilities and poetical attributes."

Proud of what was set out in the beginning and what Quill has done for the community, Lorna looks forward to seeing this book read by many "all over Scotland and maybe even round the world."

"At this time, we need hope to cling onto and Quill will be around for a long time to come. Of that I am certain."

Mary Cuerden

Mary came to writing almost by accident two years ago when asked by a friend, who had returned to West Lothian after a 10 year absence, if she would accompany her to a writers group in Craigshill.

As part of Livingston's 50 year celebrations, the group were looking for stories and poems about Craigshill.

As Mary had been among the first group of pioneers who took up residence in Craigshill in the '60s, wrote a short story called Krazy Kuts, which was then published in a small booklet called; *A Community in Words*.

The least experienced of the Quill Writers Group, Mary draws inspiration for her stories and poetry from her life experiences as a daughter, wife, mother, grandmother and recently a nana, stating; "If I can do it any one can and I hope this wee book will inspire others to take up the QUILL."

Glenn Muir

Linlithgow Postman Glenn Muir has been writing songs and poems on and off for over thirty years. Joining Quill in January 2013, Glenn writes in both Scots and English.

A Socialist, his influences include Burns, McDiarmid, Robert Service and Bob Dylan.

West Lothian Songwriters Group Songwriter of the year 2004, Glenn is also a member of folk group *Freedom's Flame*, where he plays the bodhran and the "moothie."

He currently resides in Bo'ness with his wife, Linda.

Kenneth McRae

Raised in Forres, Morayshire, Kenneth was conscripted into the Army in 1947. After demob, he went to live in Edinburgh meeting his wife Ethel, "a Leith lass," settling in Portobello for 46 years. With two sons and a daughter the family moved to Bathgate in 1999.

Kenneth began a career in Forestry/Arboriculture with the Forestry Commission in 1950, then Edinburgh Corporation and self employed until retirement at 65.

Before retiring he had no inkling that he could write poems/stories until joining a Craigmillar writers group, and under their guidance discovered, not only could he write poems/stories, but could turn his hand to art too.

Since his wife died in 2000, Kenneth has found art and writing a great comfort. Enjoying 'gigs', reading and hearing people laugh at my comedy poems. A member of various groups in Bathgate, Kenneth enjoys every one of them and continues to do so, including writing, art, and 'gigs.

Derek Cavan

Derek Cavan is a 38 year old, Bangour born poet, who adores his wife and four beautiful children.

Over the years he has participated in many different jobs including the army and the Military Police at one point.

Derek likes to take on new challenges and exert himself where possible, especially in his community.

Due to his current job – a delivery driver for the local pharmacy – Derek gets to meet many people and help them where he can. His hobbies include numerous things such as painting and poetry, feeling that he is able to express himself thoroughly through such things.

Davie Cunningham

Poetry? Whae reads it?

Or why dae folk wallow like hippos in muckle novels wi "Is that it?" endins when they cuid be lemurs galavantin across the airy branches o poetry, pluckin its choice fruits?

If ye're the sort that listens tae song lyrics, thinkin "nicely put" or "that's nailed it", there's hope for ye.

Time tae equip yersel wi a slim volume. (Like this yin! Which'll dae for sterters. Keep goin tho'!) Aw o which maybe, kindae explains why I try tae write the stuff.

Fran Thomson

Fran was brought up in Glasgow but moved to Livingston when her four children were young to make a fresh start.

She remarried in her fifties, took early retirement and moved to an old farmhouse in Kintyre, where she started to put her hobby of writing to use.

Fran has already published three books of poetry as well as numerous articles for magazines. Her fourth book is almost ready for publication.

When her husband died she came back to Livingston to be near her family. Fran has five grandchildren and three great grandchildren.

Quill Poetry and Writing Group

The Concerto ‘o Boasters

Paul Gallagher

Sitting pondering ower a jar
In this wee place we ca’ the bar
When in walks this man
Big in stature
That maks me think o’ my departure

Augustas Bassoon by name
Mare like Baboon ah wid say
Fer he had qualities like nae ither
Big ‘n’ brash wi’ voice like thunder

He wid scan the horizon wi a lengthy sweer
Then tap it aff wae a sleekit sneer
N’ tae aw in question mak’ remarks
Wi’ dugs abuse thro’ dogged bark

Aye whit a man, he thinks he’s God
And that we should worship the ground he’s trod
Nae chance ae that fer the meek should coor
But there’s those o’ us just thinks he’s soor

Bassoon belts wind around the room
As he’s paradin’ up an’ doon
Aye spoutin forth whit he has done
And the moon don’t shine where there’s nae sun

Tak’ a seat and geeze a rest, ya big baboon yer jist a pest
Ah didna say it, it wis jist a thoucht
There aff he went tae quench his throat

Aw naw look whae just came in
Silvester Trumpet tae add tae the din
Noo if oany man could blaw his ain horn
It's Silvester fer that he wis born

Tall 'n' slinky wae yon big heed
A queer lookin' shape but watch his speed
Fer he'll spit oot aboot this 'n' that
Whaur he thinks he's gawn 'n' whaur he thinks he's at

He's a flugal bugal bampot wae wee ticht lips
An' when it comes tae bragging, he'll shoot fae the hips
He'll hae ye staun at the bar
Till ye hear his last post
And then make yer ears ring wae boast boast boast

Ah really don't know wh'all survive the last bell, fer ten minutes wae Trumpet
It's just pure hell

And jist when ye think it canny get onny worse
Wae Bassoon 'n' Trumpet, noo that's the worst combination ye can get in this bar
When in she walks like some shining star
Wee Penny Whistle oh mother o' God as stuck up 'n' nippy
A richt wee sod

She'd cut ye aff above the heed, then talk ye doon till yer ears wid bleed,
Wi shrills 'n' shreeks that wid mak ye leap, ye've nae idea tae hear her peep.
Sma' 'n' fiery wae bricht carrot hair
Her skin sae smooth her face sae fair
But that wid be whaur it ends

Fer when she's angry her temper it tends
Tae (well) just go ballistic
And man, she can shout
Then turns and staunds wi her mooth in a pout

But when she's happy the Whistle it plays
'n' wae a shrill like nae ither 'n' every yin says
Penny oh Penny jist keep it doon
Then this stare and retort cuts in haulf
Tae her tune.

Aye three big egos they're a' in the room wae Whistle 'n' Trumpet and Augustas Bassoon.
Flippin' hell a quick yin then go
Thro' a gauntlet o' moothin thur stood in a row

Then aw' ae a sudden they aw' sit doon
In wan ae the corners o' this wee room
Bassoon gies a bellow a grunt at the bar
A roond fer this company and a bra fer my star
As he points tae wee Penny she laughs Ha Ha Ha.

Ah've an announcement tae mak noo we're aw here
Naw we didny just turn up tae drink a' yer beer
Wi noticed a notice tae enter a team
Fer a general knowledge quiz - said wi a grin
So Silvester and Penny, well they approached me.
And that's the team picked - aye jist us three
Silvester pips up well all being fair, we think the selection it
  is rather rare

Yer richt it is rare
Ya trumpet and a haulf
Ye micht aw be selective
Aye aw bloody daft

Noo oor wee pub canny really boast
Fer we've wan mair seconds 'n' been pipped at the post
Wi pool 'n' darts and dominoes besides and in-hoose
  disputes that hiv broken the divides

And noo they've decided tae put us oan the map
This Concerto o' Boasters
This knowledge full tap
Well thi'gither they'll staund
Or divided they'll faw
But there's yin thing fer sure
They'll still empty the hall.

Inspired by overbearing instruments out of context

Davie's Dairy Milk

Glenn Muir

Twenty fags for Pop, Turkish Delight for Maw
And a cone wi' raspberry for me.
It wis grand tae gan tae Duncan's van
In Braeheid when I wis wee.

But we forgot oor Davie's Dairy Milk
His weekly chocolate treat.
Noo he's sulkin' in the corner
Ye could almost hear him greet.

"Davie" shouts ma Faither
Davie turned his heid.
Tae gi'e a sniff fu' o' disdain
An' a look tae cut ye deid.

Weel he sat wi' his back tae us
'til oor guilty pleisures passed
O' bein' in the huff he'd had enough
Then he faced us a' at last.

He waddled o'er tae the fire
He plonked doon oan the rug
Tae sleep an' dream o' whit micht hae been
This wee fat pomeranian dug.

A Game O' Cat An' Moose

Lorna Johnston

Whit's that ye daein'
Silly Cat?
A moose, a moose
Stoap starin'
No' carin'.
Whit's that ye dae'in?
A moose, a moose
It's there
Fair game
fur the takin'
an it's quakin'
In its boots.
Silly cat
Dinnae tease it
Get yer shairp mitts oot
an seize it.
Yer saft
daft as a brush.
Ne'er seen a cat sae taken
Wi' sic a wee moose.
Dae yer worst
lang as ye dinnie hug it
Noo that wid be a mortal sin
Tae man an' beast
Sair waste o' a feast
Fur that silly cat.

Burke and Hare

Kenneth McRae

Passin Calton graveyaird the ither nicht,
Ah heard a soond an got a fricht,
The hairs stood up on the nape o' mah neck,
Ah peered through the gates just tae check,
An there, by a dimmed lantern licht,
Ah beheld a maist awfae sicht,

Twa men were diggin awa at a grave,
At that time o' nicht it wis nae way tae behave,
As ah stood an watched ah made nae soond,
As deeper an deeper, they dug intae the groond,

Yin said "Hoo far dae we hae tae go?."
The ither said "Juist another foot or so,"
As they dug deeper an deeper into the lair
Ah wis sure ah was watchin Burke an Hare
The twa grave robbers o' ill repute
Here at last were bein found oot,

It wis juist aboot then, a cat gave twa shreiks
Ah got such a fricht ah near louped oot mah breeks
But tae Burke an Hare the cat didna trouble,
They juist carried on shovellin the rubble,

At last doon the hole they were completely hid,
When ah heard the creakin o' a coffin lid,
Ah wanted tae scream an shout oot loud,
When oot the grave they came wi a shroud,

They pit the body in a big sack,
An yin pit the bundle on his back
They came towards me at the gate
Mah heart wis thumpin at a Helluva rate

Ah pushed intae the shadows as far as ah could go,
So that no' even a wee bit o' me wid show,
Ah knew if ah wis seen by that awful pair,
Ah'd end up in a sack, so ah took great care

They put the bundle on a widden barry
Tae use for their grisly load tae carry
They crept oot the kirkyaird with hardly a soond,
They looked left an right an furtively roond

They trundled the body doon the street,
Tae Knox's hoose, where him they'd meet ,
They stopped an chapped on his door,
They had obviously been there afore

They lifted the sack into the hoose,
As if it was just a bag o' refuse,

When they cam oot, in a wee while,
In the dim light ah could see them smile,
Ah was watchin them from in a stair,
When they passed that awful pair,
Sharin oot the money they had been given
Sellin bodies for the benefit o' the livin

“That was no’ bad for a night’s work,
What dae you think Mr Burke?”
“Aye, no’ bad ah suppose Mr Hare,
The morra night we’ll get some mair”,

When they had passed, ah ran awa hame,
Ah didna report it tae mah shame
Ah was scared they wid look me oot,
Whit wid happen then ah had nae doot.

But doesn’t it make ye stop an think
The lowly depths that some fowk will sink
Whit they did was certainly not funny
It’s queer what some folk will do for money.

That was the tale o’ Burke and Hare,
Ye must admit a terrible pair
Whit they did they did often,
Takin a body oot o’ it’s coffin,

Efter the corpse had been laid,
They’d come along with pick and spade,
They’d dig an dig doon the hole,
Then oot the coffin the body they stole,
It wid be cut up in a demonstration,
It was part o’ a surgeon’s education,

When at last caught by the law,
In the court they were a big draw,
Hare, he turned Kings evidence,
Though he had committed the same offence,
Burke, doon at the Grassmarket was hung,
When the rope tightened oot popped his tongue,
The fowk in the city were more than glad,
When he ended up on a dissector's slab,
What's left of him can be seen by all,
As a skeleton in the Surgeon's Hall.

Hare, he hurriedly left the town,
In case he an a' wis put down,
He went back to the Emerald Isle,
To escape goin tae the Calton Jile,

So Edinburgh got rid o' that awful pair,
That notorious duo, Burke and Hare.

It's Hard Being Eight

Christine McGhie

It's hard being eight
I'm just the child in everybody's way
Told to get lost just about every day
So I keep my head down and just get on with doing all my own stuff
Playing on my own till I've really had enough
All I want to do is hang around with them a bit more
But how can I when I'm just the youngest of four
All they ever do is tell me to leave them alone
So I trudge off to the garden to eat my ice cream cone
On my own
But it seems to me that it's not me that's daft
Because the older ones seem to think its such a big laugh
To tell me rubbish because they know I believe it
Then I'm the one in trouble and my mum is having a fit
It's hard being eight

Then it was time for tea and mum said she had something to say about my lovely old cat

And as I looked around I began to realise that he wasn't on the mat

She said he has gone to a better place than this

I thought that's nice , lucky him what bliss

So I wanted to go there too and maybe I'd find some peace

Along with my grandad because he vanished too

And no-one has phoned the police

But mum said not to be so silly,so I could still not understand

Why they had both just gone willy nilly

But mum said we would have to leave things there

And hurried me away from my chair

Because her friend Mrs Clark was coming over to embroider

And I was to be good and not to bother her

It's hard being eight

So I went off to find my big brother to see if he wanted to see Watch With Mother
But he dressed me up as a dalek from Doctor Who
And marched me outside so no tv could I view
But I was scared stiff of daleks you see
I hide behind the couch when I see them on tv
He told me if I jumped off our porch roof I could fly
But I wasn't too sure because I had never seen daleks fly
So I just began to cry
But luckily Mrs Clark came along before I could try
And he said it was all my idea and that's a lie
It's hard being eight !

So to make it up to me he said we could play one of my games
So after an argument over who got whose names
I was Illya Kuryakin to his Napoleon Solo
Off to save the world with me sucking a polo
So I was made to hide the crown jewels and some top secret papers
And I remember thinking that this seemed a right good caper
So I dug a big hole in the ground and tipped in the lot
I buried them Fast and then I was hot
The Russians will not get them there , or so I thought
Its good fun being eight !

But now my sister has come home from the big school
And once again I'm made to look the fool
Because she has lost a box that she keeps on the top of her wardrobe
And I don't know anything about that,I begin to sob
All her personal papers and trinkets so precious and dear
She keeps on shouting and I'm starting to shake with fear
Now my dad's come out and I'm starting to sense impending doom
Over the box that I have just put in a muddy tomb
And now my brothers legged it and I'm left here on my own
And I don't like the sound of my dad's tone
So I have been despatched to bed
Just as well because now I have got a sore head
And I didn't even get my nightly cup of cocoa
And he's off scot free playing with his meccano
It's hard being eight

Jean Armour

Mary Cuerden

Her name was Jean Armour she was Rabbie Burns wife
While he got all the glory she had all the strife
The day that they were married he swore to her he would be true
However it was a promise he would constantly renew

In the taverns with his cronies he wrote poems by the score
Leaving his Jeannie to keep the wolves fay the door
Each time she discovered that he had been untrue
It surely must have broken poor Jeannie's heart in two

He wrote love songs to each lassie to whom he took a fancy
How must Jean have felt when he sang of Mary,Kate and Nancy
Yet she held herself together with great dignity and pride
Even though the looks of pity were killing her inside

As Rabbie dined in Auld Reekie among the social elite
It was Jean who had to struggle to shoe their bairns' feet
He wrote of Tam O, Shanter on his horse with gleaming spurs
Jean sat at home with bairns that were all his - but not all hers

And when he lay dying it was Jeanie who was there
Administering to her husband tender love and care
So when you toast "Oor Rabbie" and celebrate his life
Remember Jeannie Armour who was oor Rabbie's wife

The Loss of a Child

May Ross

I've lost a dear child – how can I go on
My heart is in pieces – I feel my life's done
She was so very precious to me, here on earth
And how I rejoiced on the day of her birth.

I didn't know then the pain I would bear
When you took her away into your tender care
Oh! Why did you take her – I hear myself say
My sadness is bitter with each passing day.

All I can ask is 'Look after this child'
Dear Jesus. Like you, she was so meek and mild
And please for a while, till she settles to stay
Do little things for her in my special way.

She did not like the darkness in the small hours of the night
So could you, in the hallway, leave one little light
And Oh! – she liked someone to brush out her hair
Do this and the pain will be easy to bear.

I know now that my loss is your special gain
And till I cross over to meet her again
Take care of my wee one for she needs a rest
For as you will find out – she is one of the best.

A Begging Letter to Nancy

Derek Cavan

I thought I'd send a begging letter to a Lotto winner named Nancy,
I thought to myself for about five minutes to see what I would fancy.
I started by telling Nancy my shoes have holes in them.
My crazy neighbour's dog, surely has no shame.
Another thing Nancy it's really the truth,
My 19 year old lassie has a sore mouth.
She wants new teeth Nancy, oh Deary me.
It's only 5 grand Nancy, you generous wee bee.
I would rather have seen you in person, and that's the honest truth.
I'm really totally gutted, a meteorite landed though my roof.
I can't afford to fix it and my kids will surely freeze,
It's only 10 grand Nancy, I'm sure you will appease.
And finally Nancy, I'm a desperate man, and truly in despair.
My family needs a holiday and Mauritius would be rare.
Oh Nancy Nancy a begging letter is really such a sin,
Ouch my hand it really hurts the arthritis is kicking in.

My head is really buckled, and my family is getting thin,
And before I forget my Dear Nancy, my address is enclosed within.

Yours Thankfully

Derek Cavan

P.S: One last thing Nancy, you're the best you are my one true idol.
Please send me a further cheque, so I can shop in Lidl.

The Aldi Blues

Fran Thomson

A needed some milk so a went oan doon tae Aldi's
It wis full o' the 'Blue rinse brigade' an the Baldys
A' wi' the same idea – tae try an save a copper
Wi' 'Buy wan, get wan free' ye felt ye'd found a whopper
A stertit tae pick up tins o' this an' bits o' that
Loads o' different things tae feed tae ma wee cat
Written in Chinese it wis awfy hard tae tell
Jist whit wis inside – wis it good or did it smell?

At the checkout a mither wis sortin oot hur purse
Anither wan wis yellin, 'Hey, a wis in here furst!'
The weans a' hud a battle while the till went 'ting-a-ling'
It looked like this wee wumin hud wan o' everything
When it came tae ma turn a wis ta'en aback
A'd bocht things that a don't eat, like tatties in a sack
Biscuits, cakes an' sweeties, things a didny need
I hudny goat the milk, the butter ur the breed!!

The money haunded o'er I pit them in the car
Then hame intae the kitchen – it wisny very far
Ma wee cat widny eat the food that a pit doon
It wis screechin' at the dug so a hit it wi' a spoon
A'm no goin' back tae Aldi's, a felt it wis a sin
Maist o' whit a bocht hus landed in the bin!
A bargain's no a bargain if ye dinny need it
Dinny look at stuff if ye know ye canny read it

Jist get whit ye know yer really gonny use
That'll help tae chase awa the 'Aldi Blues'!

A Ferry Sets Sail

Davie Cunningham

Jist a shoogle in traditional holiday routine – but in sic a wey life's changing patterns are signalled. Alsae a tribute tae oor delicately devastatin Scots word fir 'lost' – 'tint'.

Relinquishin, release, surrender
Sair or poignant, done, relief,
A fist that grups hard wi tendons strainin *grips*
Opens at last – and aw is tender-
As loss o strain allows new pain in :
Yince a life-line's haudit there's nae prief *prevention*

Against this stingin paradox *sad/tear-causing*
Which ay yerks us unaware… *tugs at/wrenches*
Like when yer swim towel needit foldin
For dooks in future pools and lochs
An there's me greetin – Ah'd nae warnin
-Jist at the thocht o no bein there.

An sae we stuid upon the pier *so*
Primed for wavin as ye sailed
It wis bye-bye tae a grand tradition
We'd nurtured for a guid ten year.
Auld weys fade – but nivir this yin!
Yet a jug brim-fu is easy skailt. *spilled*

Sea fine an smooth, sun up an shinin
Yacht lets slip – an disappears-
No monie folk for this mornin's ferry
Pier repair chaps sawin and grindin
Veteran fairweel-ers, fairly merry.
It's time for feelin an time for tears.

Quick question tae a handy crewman
Ower the gang plank, there ye are!
Sclimmed nimble tae the upper viewin deck *climbed*
Wavin ower the gowden blue calm
Whaur antrin currents intersect, *opposing*
As thae douce, fierce engines gently jar. *pleasant/likeable*

And och, it's fine, it's richt an fine –
Onwart, ye skelf o starflint! *onwards*
Flee soarin on yer ain trajectory *fly*
Frae gravities which we'll resign.
Joyous lowsin! Awbody's victory! *setting free*
Nae teary slitter, oor een unblint. *unblinded*
Jist a ferry sailed – an something tint. *lost*

Culloden Field 16 April 1746

Kenneth McRae

On a morn that wis dreich, cauld an sodden
Baith armies met on that field at Culloden,
The King's army advanced slowly ower the peat,
They slithered step by step by the drum beat.

True Highlanders, rugged men with axe an sword.
Were ready tae meet the advancin Redcoat horde
Cannon rained doon whaur the clans-men stood,
Oot-numbered, whit chance had they in the feud,
Against cannon an scatterin grape,
The brave Highlanders had nae escape,

Intae the peat blood noo begins tae seep,
Blood o the clansmen, sinkin dark an deep,
A' they had wis sword, targe an dirk,
But against the Redcoats they didna shirk,
Sworn tae fight for Bonnie Prince Charlie,
Wi the enemy there wis tae be nae parley.
They wid aw fight tae the death,
Their blood spillin on the earth,

The English army loomed oot the fog,
The clans stood steadfast in the bog.
How mony were slaughtered on an off that field?
We'll never ken - but if it ever is revealed

Then the wanderin o' oor brave men will surely cease,
An their brave souls will at last rest in peace.

Glorified Tiddlywinks!

Glenn Muir

Glorified bluidy tiddlywinks.
Hardly a sport, mair o'a game,me thinks.
Fuils an' dafties yin and aa
They skelp then hunt a wee white ba.

Gowf, the scoundrel's last resort
Me, I'd hunt the bluidy lot
Wi' thir talk o' birdies an' o' eagles
They deserved tae be chased by a pack o' beagles

Aa in thir fancy gear,bespoke
Luik doon thir nose at common folk
Bit wha are they tae show disdain?
They are posers, in the main

Noo, if a gowfer hits a blinder
Nae hook, nae slice, nae arsehole-winder
Straucht doon the middle, whit a thrill
It wis mair tae dae wi' luck than skill

When at last, the roond is done
It's intae the club-hoose for some fun
These blawhard braggarts I cannae thole
They play thir best at the nineteenth hole.

Bird Brain

Derek Cavan

I thought I saw a Cheshire cat,
The wee adamant Scots budgie said.
The look it got in return,
Was enough to render it dead.
With steadfast mind and straight up spine,
The budgie stood its ground.
The Cheshire cat looked it straight in the eye, And said,
"you are due me a pound."
The wee Scots budgie gave out a smile,
The cat was in a rage.
The wee bird said, "You want your pound,
It's on the floor of my cage."
The Cheshire cat said, "Is that right,
You want to play games, you've done it now.
Tonight I'm coming to rattle your cage."
The Scots budgie said, "Oh is that right?
I think you'll find that's wrong."
Because tonight you're off to the cattery,
And me and your pound's going to uncle Tom's.

A Passion For Poetry

Lorna Johnston

A passion for poetry is such
That the time spent is never too much
You write it and tweak it and turn it around
It's a comfort for many I've found.
There is humour, emotion and even true life
There is rhyming, non rhyming and trouble and strife
There are sad ones and bad ones and even the worst
Can turn round and bite you and give you a thirst
To bring words together in your own special way
And many more thoughts that have come into play.
They say that love is a choice we all make
My love is poetry a claim I will stake
My heart and my life, till the end of time
I am a passionate wordsmith of poetical rhyme.

Clootie Dumplin'

Fran Thomson

Me an ma man wur watchin the telly
When he says tae me, "A've a rumbly belly
A fancy a treat like a cake ur a scone
Will you mak me sumthin? No jist tea oan its own."
A packet o' scone mix wis up oan the shelf
So a stertit tae mix it in there by maself
When in comes auld rumbly looking quite doon
"The telly is rubbish – here, gie me that spoon"

A asked could he bake and he answered "Aye,
Ma Granny showed me when a wis so high"
A jist stood and watched as he pulled oot the stuff
The kitchen wis littered an a'd hud enough
So a left him to it - that wis a mistake
A should hiv known that he couldny bake
He pit flour, fruit an sugar into this mix
Two pints o' watter, four crushed weetabix

He kept pittin mair in – a said wi a sigh,
"Whit ur ye makin, a cake ur a pie?"
"It wis gonny be scones bit it didny look right
Then a sponge wi some fruit wis fur your delight
A've pit in some spices, an things frae the press
A know that the kitchen's a bit o' a mess
Bit this dumpling will be the nicest ye've seen
A promise it will be fit fur a queen!"

Intae a slip he poured this big plaster
A should hiv known it wid end in disaster
Then intae the pressure pot boilin an hissin
A did try tae tell him bit he widny listen!
Ten minutes later we heard this great "Whoof!"
There wis durty brown watter a' oer the roof
Ye couldny get in tae turn aff the heat
It ran doon the wa's and wis under wur feet

A towel wrapped roon so he didny burn
He goat in and gave the gas tap a turn
When it a' settled an cooled doon a bit
A wis quite grateful an thought "Weel, that's it!"
Bit no – in the microwave went this big blob
Came oot like a boulder, a thought "Jist the job"
We wur needing sumthin tae haud the back door
While he painted the kitchen and scrubbed a' the floor!

A New Baby

May Ross

This child is sent for you to love
He's sent to you from God above
And Heavens Angels made him sweet
So they could lay him at your feet.

He is your bright and shining star
To cherish here and not afar
He'll bring you joy – I'm sure you know
As from you both this love will flow.

His tiny hands, his chubby cheeks
You'll watch throughout the coming weeks
You'll gaze in wonder at his face
As he grows up in God's good grace.

Teach him all the tiny things
Like why a butterfly has wings
And why the Lord made good and bad
And why there's happy and there's sad.

But most of all teach him to care
Through all lives trials, wear and tear
For that's God's message sent through him
So keep it and it won't grow dim.

He must be very special too
For God to give him to you
And through the years you'll watch him grow
The Holy Spirit through him flow.

So hold your wee one close and near
For to you both he's very dear
And through this love he'll grow each day
To love and care in every way.

Dave The Post Scot

Kenneth McRae

He delivered mail tae but and ben
Tae his Lordship in his castle
He took his job seriously
Tae him it wis nae hassle

Though he never left his hills or glen
He'd travelled the world wide
Lookin at the picture postcairds
An words on the ither side.

He delivered his mail from near an far
Africa, America and even one fae Pitcairn
Even though it wisnae part o' his job
He's been known to deliver some wifie's bairn

When snow is thick on the ground
An he cannae use his bike
He'd put his wellies on
Leave his bike an hike

He's never known tae be off sick
Went oot in aw kinds o' weather
An if he'd hae a minute tae spare
He'd hae a cup o' tea an a blether

Davie never married, said he has nae time
But ye never saw him sad
There's a wee laddie in the glen
Awfae like Davie, his dad?

When Davie died they didnae bury him
As he'd done his duty wi great pride
Folk built a stone cairn wi a big slot
An posted him inside

If ever you're up that glen
An ye think yer lost
On a hill ye'll find a cairn
Beside it, a postie ghost

Don't be scared, he'll no' bother ye
Dinna run awa an hide
It's just old Davie the post
Deliverin messages fae the ither side.

Me and Billy

Mary Cuerden

Me and my best pal Billy wanted to be soldiers ever since we were weans
There was nothing we liked better than playing yon patriot games
Running and hiding in the woods with oor wooden guns
Me and my best pal Billy just had so much fun

Me and my best pal Billy noo long after we left the schuil
Went and joined the army even thought there was nay one we wanted to kill
Me and my best pal Billy in our uniform thought we looked braw
But my best pal Billy's brother telt me and Billy "we had nay brains at aw"

Me and my best pal Billy's Sergeant was a Glasgow man called Ken
He telt me and Billy that he turn laddies into men
Me and my best pal Billy training aw complete
Knew as Scottish soldiers we numbered among the elite

Me and my best pal Billy were sent to a place called Afghanistan
To stop terrorism and oppression we had to fight the Taliban
Me and my best pal Billy were sent out on patrol
To keep the highway open was me and Billy goal

Suddenly there was a flash and a pain I could nay bare
Me and my best pal Billy were flying through the air
The last thing I remember was an awful thudding sound
It was me and my best pal Billy landing on the ground

Someone called for a medic who came and shook his heid
And said that he wis sorry but "I am afraid that they're both deid."
Me and my best pal Billy were pit into a bag
From there into a coffin which they covered with a flag

When we arrived in Wotton Basset people lined the street
Me and my best pal Billy's mothers could do nothing else but greet
They played Flowers of the Forest as they lowered us into oor grave
And oor commanding officer said me and Billy had been brave.

And that our names would be written on the great wall of fame
But me and my best pal Billy just wished we stayed at hame

The Whisperin' Win'

Glenn Muir

The gentle win' frae o'er the Forth
It whispers, "Come tae me"
A longing stirs within my hert
The Ochils for tae see
Tae go and tread they ancient hills
Then the mountains, North and West
Tae ken an' better unnerstaun
This lan' that I lo'e best

I hae this yearnin' deep within
An endless gnawin' need
Tae seek oot auld Alba's ancient ways
Frae St.Abbs tae Dunnet Heid
Tae stroll beneath a Saltire sky
In ablaw a Scottish sun
Tae hear the wild geese high above
An' watch the rivers run

I hear the saugh o' the whisperin' win'
It draws me oot the door
I'll pit my best fit tae the road
Like a thoosan times afore
Awa tae they high an' wild hills
Whaur the air is fresh an' clear
Jist me masel an' the lonesome win'
An' the runnin' o' the deer

Hush, Little One

Fran Thomson

Hush now, little one – not a sound,
there are people all around
Hear the horses gallop by,
listen to the hue and cry
All that barking, my sweet son
means a fox is on the run
Such a panic he must feel,
danger chasing at his heel

We must lie here very still
else the pack will treat us ill
Not a rustle must we make
or our cover we will break
I don't know the how or why
men feel foxes have to die
But I do know, darling one,
that could be us on the run

All we ask is peace to live,
to eat what God and land can give
To wander free in fields and wood
with plentiful supplies of food
Of man we ask nothing at all,
he lives behind his strong brick wall
Someday perhaps the hunt will cease
and we can live our lives in peace

But until then the lesson learn,
hide down deep in grass and fern
For guns and dogs and people too
would be the death of me and you.

The Tradesman

Paul Gallagher

As the tradesman knocked on his client's door
His client walked through halls and floors
To warily glance from the outstretched door
Then glanced again her spotless floor.

''Well there's a backdoor at the other side''
With glare and stare, with household pride
So lifts her head to point the way
Her tradesman knows to walk that way

Now to show this man her troubled spot
Well, boots on carpet he must not
So leave them out behind the door
With socks on feet he knows the score

Now led with such an inquisitive pace
For not too fast for not to race
For a steadfast job required thought
There hands and mind together brought

''Well here we are it's in your hands
This troubled spot may need new plans
To fix it right, to make it new
Oh tradesman, it's now up to you''

So with paper he did size the spot
Of which his client she has fraught
To all he had to satisfy
Make good and right for this he'll try

''Oh please make sure your sheets are clean to
   cover up my suites of cream
My halls and carpets miss your boots with
   mud and oil or rust or soot
Then all debris, well it must go into a bag
That you can throw into a skip and out of
   sight
No dusty bowl, no reckless blight''.

So he reassures his client dear
No dust or grime she'll have to fear
For cover up and dust it down would take
   away his client's frown

''Well that would be the price you'd pay
By cheque or cash or other ways''
The client looked a worried look
As eyes ran down the tradesman's book

''A hefty sum I have to say
Of which or how or would I pay''

''By cheque or cash or other ways''
''What do you mean?''

The tradesman says with eyes a beam
''You may well earn reduction rates
For service rendered you'd be paid''

Confused now client in a state
Near shows her tradesman to the gate
But still intrigued to shorten quote or place hands round this
tradesman's throat

'Well spit it out and make it clear
This other way it sounds quite queer'

The tradesman laughs and says 'I see
Reduce your bill and work for me

Tidy up behind my back, make my lunch and fill the sack
Polish boots to make them clean
Then dust your halls and make them beam
Of that I know you would be great'

At that the tradesman saw the gate.

Summit Fever

Christine McGhie

Beware of the man that's got summit fever
He is going to the top at whatever the cost
These powerful men with such charisma, genius and Flair
They render your common sense lost
Such a potent heady form of attraction
But with them there will be no satisfaction
You need to keep them out of your head and your heart
Keep yourself free
Because the reality that lurks beneath is far less
Attractive you see
You'll get trampled on underfoot
They will suck the life out of you ,to boot
Because inside they are emotionally dead
And sadly girls they are usually useless in bed
They think of nothing and no-one but themselves
And dump you when the no longer want you
Without so much as a backward glance
And then move on swiftly to pastures new
Beware of the man that's got summit fever
He will leave you damaged forever.

Hunkert

Davie Cunningham

Hunkert he hauds the handle, fingers damp,
Accusin heroes striding thro' his brain
Maw's read him monie stories o the deeds
O men whae faced up danger, feared nae pain.

Wersh licht, strang soon, come thro' the door's thin crack. *thin/sour*
The hoarse, coorse dunner o the villain's curse
The prayerful pleadin o the lady's cry.
Lug sair against door's edge he waits fir worse.

An he cin see a Bold Boy breengin doon
Wi sheer velocity an virr he cowps *energy*
The bad guy whae, shamed wi this moral dunt,
Shrinks as ower him the hero lowps.

And oh, the grateful glow in lady's ee
The battlefield that's flitted frae her face
Nivir again, no ivir, will she greet
Her gaze tells Boy she's in a better place.

An then, the first skelp, hard haun on soft cheek
Next it's the scream, the soond he cannae bear
Frae neb an mooth bluid soon will stert tae seep
Some will coagulate in strands o hair.

The Heroboy sneers at him in the draucht *draught*
Presses cauld hannle deep intae his broo
Against bent, yisless knees the cairpet drags
His flighterin hert flaffs like a scruntit doo. *flaps like a weak pigeon*

In short months he'll resent her victim's role
Find reasons tae excuse his drunken dad.
That's us. We'll dig obscure richt ootae wrang
Then fash awa at why the warld seems mad.

But he's appeasin heroes: airmoured minds
Hard muscles, mystic maucht an perfect timin *might*
They're no there tae sort oot a life that's murlt *messed up*
By conscience dirlin its continuous mindin

But aw the courage that he needs tae learn
Is tae look back, admit, alloo hissel *allow himself*
Tae say that he's on this vertiginous ledge
Whaur he's been set tae tend his special hell.

Insteid years pass, his dad awa, then deid,
As he tries lives he nivir cin abide
An she lives fir wee stories o his daeins
An baith must thole things that their minds must hide.

Atween them rins this ceaseless drumlin causie. *street*
There's yit a chance tae dodge its chains o traffic
An find it's thrang wi life, benign an busy
A keen-tae-be deciphered hieroglyphic.

Whit champ will kittle up his jinkin courage? *stir up*
Imagination needs tae find yin noo
Tae say, " Rise frae yer knees an gently, touch her.
"Trummle, blether, feel faint … be brave, be true." *tremble*

Gordon Ramsay and Me

Kenneth McRae

Who taught Gordon to make guid tea?
Confidentially, it wis me
It's no' like me ah dinna like to boast
Ah also taught him how to make toast
Ah never used to curse an swear
He taught me, so there
He went on to do better things
Cookin for Emperors an Kings

Ah like too cook, ah really do
Fancy myself as a Cordon Bleu
Lookin for work an for a laugh
Ah got myself a job in a caff
Jist an ordinary 'greasy spoon'
Hopin a better job would come soon
We didna cook high falutin fancy stuff
In fact the grub an the place was a bit rough
In spite o' this the café was veryclean
The owner believed in good hygiene

Caterin in that caff was a bit slap-dash
A' kinds o' sandwiches an corned beef hash
Some o' the sandwich fillins were queer
But they sold fast as they weren't dear
Fish dipped in bread crumbs or gooey batter
Ony way ye liked it, it didn't really matter
Served with salt, sauce, chips an peas
Oor aim was the customers to please
It looked good, appetisin an great
Wrapped in paper or on a plate

We served a' kinds o' fried food
Some o' it crap, some o' it good
Get dug in wi a knife an fork
Eat the meal, dinna talk
An when ye've finished yer meal
Ye will admit it wis a guid deal
Maybe ah should gaun oot on a limb
Curse an swear just like him
But ah liked tae keep mah kitchen staff calm
Me! Curse an swear' well! Maybe a wee damn

That's mh story ended, can it be all true?
Ah left that caff, became a Cordon Blue
Most of ye ken me, ah dinae tell lies
Ah'm much better at makin porky pies

So if yer wantin a guid meal at five star hotel do
Give me a call, ah'll bring along mah pal Gordon too
In our scrumptiously clean whites we'll be there
Ye hae tae hae bags o' money or be a millionaire
Ye'll have tae be, tae meet oor cost
If yer no', dinna phone me, get lost

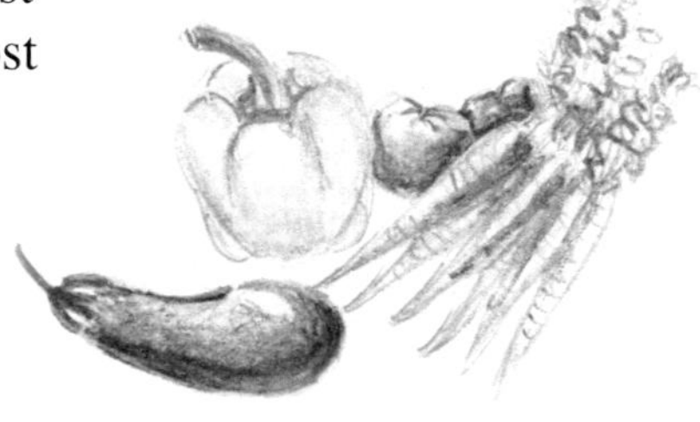

A Cannae Write a Poem

Derek Cavan

A cannae write a poem,
A hate masel sae much.
Ither folk's poems rhyme,
bit a am oot o touch.

Av tried tae string a sentence,
Bit ma brain jist wullnae work.
A dinnae ken how am writing this,
Ma heid is fit tae burst.

Am sorry fur the boredom,
Ma brain should work quite soon.
Ah'll hopefully huv some poem ideas,
And git them written doon.

Memories of Mothers Day

Mary Cuerden

It will have to be a secret I heard my eldest daughter say
We will make Mum breakfast and put it on a tray
We haven't got any money for a present or a card
I am sure we could make one it can't be all that hard
Her brother and her sister with excitement clapped their hands
Then the three put their heads together and started making plans
The very next morning I had to pretend to be asleep
When my three children into my bedroom creep
"Happy Mothers Day surprise surprise surprise"
And I try to look startled as I open up my eyes
I use my elbow to slowly raise my head
While three pairs of hands fluff the pillows in my bed
Very carefully they placed a tray down by my side
Their three little faces were so full of joy and pride
They handed me a piece of paper carefully folded into two
And said Mummy we made this card specially for you
And as I opened it my tears I could not hide
As I read the words that they had written there inside
"To the world's best Mother we love you very much"
And a hundred kisses was their finishing little touch
Now if the truth about that breakfast was ever to be told
The toast it was burnt and the porridge it was cold
The coffee was full of floating little bits
But I would not have swapped it for dinner at the Ritz
Now they are grown when ever we're apart
The memory of that breakfast is forever in my heart

An Ode Tae The Sun

May Ross

Ah looked oot o' mah windae
An' there tae mah surprise
The sun was shinin' – whit a treat –
Lightin' up the skies.

That day ah had intended
Tae wash mah kitchen flair
But the sun wis oot – so stuff if
And ah headed up the stair.

Tae find mah wee bikini
But where – ah couldnae remember
Ah wore it last time the sun wis oot
Aye – that wis last September.

Ah finally found it – it wis braw
But ah had tae try and keep calm
For when ah tried it oan
It was mair like mutton than lamb.

But ah couldnae waste the sunshine
A pair o' shorts wid dae
But dearie me there wis nae a pun' o' me
Hingin' jist the richt way.

So ah get oot a wee T-Shirt
And then a hud a notion
Afore ah go ah need somethin' else
A bottle o' sun lotion.

It wis quite a while, I know
Since I had used it last
And when ah got it opened
Its 'use by date' wis past.

Noo aw' this frantic searchin'
Left me feelin' rather weak
An' ah wis puffin an' pantin
An' mah skin wis beginnin' tae leak.

So ah laid a towel oan the grass
Hopin' ah widnae burn
Then a wee bitty cloud covered the sun
Aw, Jings – it's oan the turn.

Mair clouds noo gaithered
Thunder rolled like a speedin' train
Ah should've washed mah kitchen flair
Fur noo it's rainin' again.

Troglodyte

Glenn Muir

It's grand tae be a Troglodyte
And wear the skins o'thaim thit bite
Noo we aa bide in a cosy cave
(Whaur yince thir dwelt a bear ca'd Dave)

We cam alang an' smoked'm oot
We killed 'm deid withoot a doot
We skinned then cooked'm oan the fire
Despite his angst, despite his ire

Bear soup, bear roast and then bear stew
Bear thermidor an' bear ragout
Whit wis left we smoked like kippers
Dave's hide made the hale tribe's slippers

Though we ate'm in a hurry
Three weeks later it wis still bear curry
We've nivir yince ate bear again
(We've lived oan takeaways since then)

Losing Weight

Fran Thomson

I read in the paper about this diet
It looked so good that I thought I'd try it
All the salads and things were bought
Looked at cakes but said, "Better not."

When I got home the whole family
Gave me their advice for free
"Walk the dog three times a day
And all the flab will fade away."

Another said that I should jog
Every day rain, sun or fog
This would make me feel much better
Even if I did get wetter!

An exercise bike was quickly bought
Then weights – I really had the lot
I'd no excuse, I had to try
To get a figure slim and spry.

I stuck this torture for many weeks
Admittedly I had rosy cheeks
But I didn't lose a single pound
Though I jogged myself into the ground

So I gave up, I'm still quite plump
My shape has many a funny bump
It's just the way I'm meant to be
And I'm quite happy just being me!

A Great Nicht Wis Had By Aw

Lorna Johnston

A great nicht oot
It wis sae guid
An' atmosphere
Wis as it shuid
be; it wis classic.
Joab weel done
An' everyboady
Hid sae much fun.
Noo Davy
he wis oan the ball
Words pitch perfect
Ne'er did stall.
His shairp renditions
Interludes
O' Glenn Millars hit
Goat us 'in the mood'.
He shair wis crazy
A special treat
Ye couldnie get him
Back tae his seat.
Held awe the folk
In palm o' haun
An' captivated
Socked it tae 'em
Really grand.
An' then cam Paul
Whaw weaved his magic
'Ah'm comin' hame'
Wis really tragic.
This brought a tear

Tae oor Fran's eye
Or mebbe that wis
They twa flies.
Bit Paul, he did dae really weel
Wi'feather in his hat
His presentation skills
Ne'er fell flat.
In fact!
He wis a winner up there
Tellin' all
Wi' aw the recitations
He managed tae recall.
Paul tae a tee
Shairp an' prepared
Nothing ever
Makes him scared.
An' as fur Fran
Whit kin ye say
Her repertoire
Made aw folk's day.
Staunin' confident she wis
An' every funny anecdote
Ye really couldnie miss.
She kens her trade.
Audience were beguiled
Belted them oot
In her ain unique style.
Couldnie stoap laughin'
Wi' sides fit tae burst
An' countless innuendoes

Tae gie folk a thirst
fur more.
Last bit not least
Kenny proved to all here
He's a force tae be reckoned wi'
Nae fear.
Waited patient and quiet
An'gave o' his best
Then went back and sat doon
Tae a well earned rest.
Comin' back he wis brilliant
The second time roond
Goat aff tae a flyin' stairt
Feet ne'er touched the groond.
Wi' Goldilocks, Red Riding Hood
Sic really funny stories
Mixed up wi' a patter
That made them sae gory.
Bit whit the heck
It's modern times
An' Kenny the Poet
Made it all sound sublime.
A great nicht fur aw
Happy memories an' more
Here's tae next year
An' whit lies in store.

My Mistress Of Strategy

Glenn Muir

She's my Mistress of strategy, she reads the signs well.
None can fool or cajole her nor lies to her, tell
She doesn't knit jumpers or darn old socks
She learned about life, in the school of hard knocks
She's my Mistress of Strategy

She's my Mistress of Strategy, she's my eyes and my ears
Keeping me safe from life's troubles and fears
What you see's what you get, what you get's what you see
Conquered my heart, oft times saved me from me
She's my Mistress of Strategy

She's my Mistress of Strategy, she'd be brilliant at chess
There's no ambush or pitfall she can't second guess
Her spirit, proud and free - never suffers a fool
Am I the exception or merely the rule?
She's my Mistress of Strategy.

Childhood

Derek Cavan

I thought I would write a poem this day,
With childhood my theme, what can I say?

Bangour General is where it all began,
On January the tenth nineteen seventy five.

Brought home to Boghall where all was grand,
We were once surrounded by lovely farmland.

Sometimes a bus would take us away,
Where are we going mum? Portobello she'd say.

School was quite good I can't complain,
Even though my teacher said I only had half a brain.

An altar boy I was deemed to be,
My grandma knew the Bishops so that was it for me.
Hair combed to the side on a Sunday,
And all the way up Limefield Hill.
My pals had a good laugh at me,
But I thought I was brill.

My dad he kept budgies,
And we had rabbits too.
We had a cat that ran away,
Obviously couldn't handle the zoo.

The Patter of Tiny Feet

Christine McGhie

Tian Tian's thirty six hour breeding window came and went
Fruitless hours watching the pandas the keepers spent
On getting her pregnant they were hell bent
But she simply wasn't interested in Yang Guang's scent
So they took desperate measures and they gave her IVF
The donor was a dead german panda so to keep him anonymous lets call him Jeff
But what is so puzzling to me is if pandas all over the world don't like having sex at all
How on earth have they survived from ancient times when they built the great china wall
Maybe they just like privacy, peace and space and to choose their own partner like everyone else
And now the waiting game is on to see if her tummy swells
A new baby panda for Scotland next year, a new young scot
Well Alex Salmond will really love that
A new baby panda for an SNP mascot
Just the tonic to get our ailing economy back on track
From all over the world to Edinburgh Zoo people will flock
But you never know it might even be twins
Now that would really be a win win
Photo opportunities galore with the new born on his knee
A cue for us to pander to Alex and vote for the SNP
And a historic new way of life for you and me

Jungle of Memories

Kenneth McRae

Clydebank, silent, forgotten,
The foundry, the shipyards, dead.
Streams of molten steel, motionless.
No more sculptured great ships.
The planners, tradesmen, the engineers, lives destroyed
Men moulding, stretching, twisting, now unemployed

The laying down of the keel,
Wee men, in dungarees, greasy bunnet, flat,
Building famous ships, steel pinned to steel,
The gaffer, with his bowler hat,

The clank and clanging of the riveters noise,
The good natured laugh at a dirty joke,
The shouts and swearing at the tea boys,
Fun at each other these hardy men poke.

Sitting together having their "piece."
Won't matter if their hands are all grease.
Where are all these hardy folk?
Gone forever in a jungle of memories.

Seterday, pey day, in fur a pint an a nip,
Whisky, water o' life, hae a wee sip,
Or swallay them baith quickly doon,
A nip an a pint, for half a croon,
Needid that, whit ither pleasures dae ah seek?
Efter workin bloody hard a' week.
Oan the dugs, a tanner each way,
Loast, ach well, there's eiwis anither day,
Nae yis greetin ower spult mulk,
Nae yis moanin, goin in the sulk,
A tanner doon the drain,
Nae new baffies fur the wean,

A row fae the wife. "Ye wee nyaff, ya slob,
Hoo kin ah manage oan one an fifty bob,
Hoo ah'm tae manage ah dinna ken,
Tae run this run doon but an ben."

Where are all these hardy folk?
Gone forever in a jungle of memories

What's happened to all that inborn gift?
Generations of Grand-dads, fathers, sons,
Where are these hard, rough, tough men?
Who sculpted elegance from raw steel,
And fashioned it into ships of splendour,
In every steel plate, bolt and rivet
Blood, sweat and tears, curses, pride.
Steel monuments to Clydebank, Glasgow,

But alas no more, men and ships, rusting,
Cast aside on the waves of time,
WHERE HAS IT ALL GONE?
Gone for-ever, in a jungle of memories.

Clones

Fran Thomson

When I heard the news it gave me a start
Instead of just taking bodies apart
Doctors and scientists now have a way
To make human beings – and not out of clay
With test tubes and chemicals, DNA strands
They can even make people a new pair of hands
Grow skin and kidneys to make people well
Transplant an organ and hope it will gel

These things are wonderful, this I am sure
Diseases wiped out now they have a cure
But where will it end? I haven't a clue
Dolly the sheep caused enough of a stew
Will we be able to order a child
Lovely blonde hair and temperament mild?
Clever and honest, a real pride and joy
"What would you like – a girl or a boy?"

Queue up like the Co-op on dividend day
Wait for the man at the counter to say,
"Where's Mrs Baldwin to collect her three
We have a sale on – buy two – get one free!"
If you don't like the one that you mother
Will they exchange it and give you another?
I think there are some things best left alone
What happens to someone who is a clone?

Man is not God - He is the Master
I feel that we humans now flirt with disaster!

Fighting Winter

May Ross

Cold winter with her sparkling gown
Encrusted with shining jewel.
Her beauty takes your breath away
But it hides a heart so cruel.

Oh! Winter with her cold white dress
Is a pleasure you'll want to keep.
But touch it not or you will find
That beauty's just skin deep.

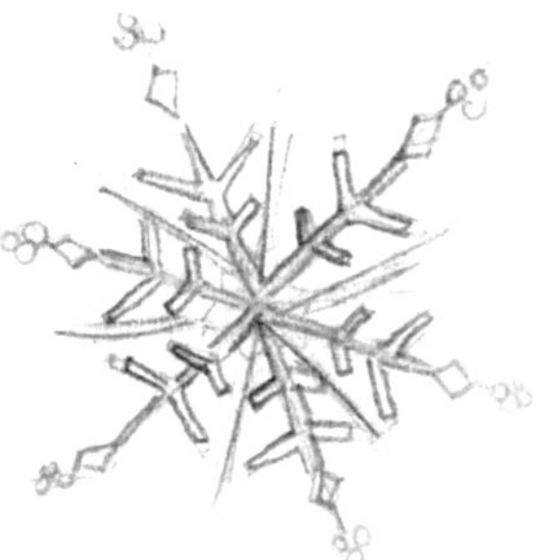

For when her frosty needles sharp
Point their fingers at your heart
You'll see her glossy glittering cloak
An evil festering wart.

Her majesty holds mountains high
Tight within her grasp
And even rivers and valleys green
Can never escape her clasp.

Her mighty talons grip and squeeze
The life-blood from all nature
Her power expends a fearful force
O'er every man and creature.

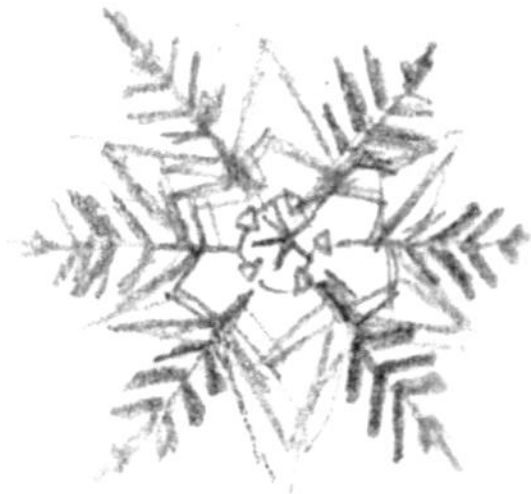

But soon her strength begins to wane
She's met her foe at last.
For spring wakes up from her resting place
And roars a mighty blast.

She blows life-giving, soft, sweet winds
To chase the evil round us
The gentle rain to melt her heart
And the sun once more has found us.

Farewell, evil thorn in the countryside
You sag and your strength grows weak
For we think spring is gentle but with one single blow
She can tear you apart – who says she is meek?

So sleep, wicked one for you'll need you all your power
To fight all three seasons too
So till we meet again when these battles have done
Mighty winter may I salute you.

Fireworks

Lorna Johnston

Bang!
Went the firework
Weaving through the sky
The poor wee frightened woman
Was heard to screech and cry.
Just as the firework came to rest
Upon her sorry head
She ran around and back again
Fell to the ground near dead.
They carried her away so fast
Her face was white as chalk
People setting fireworks off
Stopped by to have a gawk.
The ambulance came quick and fast
And screeched up to a halt
When another firework seen to fall
Was really no ones fault.
The woman got an awful fright
While lying on the stretcher
She jumped back off and ran away
So fast, no one could catch her.
The moral of the story is
To never venture out
Especially on fireworks night
Cause you'll hear an eerie shout.
The spirit of the woman floats
About that street where she
Was struck down with a firework
And that woman
SHE WAS ME!!

The Lost Lintie

Glenn Muir

Blue cornflowers mind me of you
All tender in the morning dew
And linties taking to the wing
It's with your voice I hear them sing

Weel I remember wine and craic
The memories they take me back
A jest,a story and a sang
Drove monies a merry nicht alang

I've seen the nicht but noo it's day
The simmer blossoms fade away
Nae lintie sings within these wa's
We're left wi nocht but craws and daws

Yet come the day an'come the hour
We'll hear the lintie's sang once more
Ablaw fair Eden's morning dew
Blue cornflowers will bloom anew.

The Autumn Storm

Paul Gallagher

As cold wind blows oer hallowed graves
There heavy boot hits weary spade
Light disappears behind grey skies
The rustling chestnut tree, it sighs

Black crow craws from swaying branch
As wind and crows engage in dance
For now slowbrook it runs so fast
No solace for the angler cast

He crunched the leaves by path by woods
That runs with colours, autumn moods
The silent whispers from the brush
The spirit blows its breath says hush

Heart beats hard as heart beats fast
As dusk does fall as day does pass
Then rain brings in the night so dark
And all remains lamenting lamp
To shed some light for him to tramp

Through country lanes as hedges sway they
Push to shove to point the way
Backs to the wind then bustling on
The waning moon alas has gone

A tired and creaking gate it kicks, its cottage
walls, its deep red bricks
Eyes now catch a glowing, flickering light
Through window panes a welcomed sight

So step inside the warmth to face
Sweet smell from garlic's nose to trace
Remove damp heavy jacket hanged
Not by the noose but metal fanged
Then sank into the mucker's chair
No weather here no season's care
Embraced an autumn hot broth gold
Supped back to take away the cold.

Still cold the wind shakes strong from gale
On hallowed graves now sheds its hail
The long and lonely grave there fills
As mud from water sheds the hill
Brown pools now level overflows,
The pitted ground where flowers grow
Tall thick gates groaned from rust
Then shudder with the winds that burst

Deep inside brick cottage walls
So warm, so snug, tired eyes now fall
Fall drowsy, only ears awake,
As wind on tiled roof there quakes
The warmth now comforts weary bones
From hard resilient stricken stones
Repeat, repeat, damned kicking gate
As ears now turning off, so hate
Retreat below the covers soft
They dampen sounds outside aloft
then drift off gently silent dreams.
A differential world it seems.

As tick tock ticking clock ticks on
The raging storm outside fights on
As carnage reaps twigs fly around
As cracking trees fall to the ground
Crisp leaves all dancing to the tune
Storms whistle blows impending doom
And there lone cottage lies in wait.

BANG

A catastrophic CRASHING sound as ripping roots tear from the ground
His slumbered body there lay still
A branch had speared its fatal kill
Then storm swept through to take his soul
To leave four walls an empty hole
No mercy shown to all in wake
No foot put on its mighty brake
For break and rip with earthward bounds
Shook woods their neck's aggressive pounds

Then hailed on all that lay below
The hallowed grave, the blackest crow
The lonely cottage shell so brave
Did try to shelter, failed to save
The long lost lonely grave would fill
From heavy boot the storm had killed
To fill from his own hands
There lay in wake from storm was damned

Dark wet hole take these bones
Take thy soul
Cover thee the autumn leaf
To camouflage thy hidden grief
Cover thee and comfort still
To lay out here this storm's will
Craw black crow then sit, be still
Don't dance the storm's bitter pill.

As daybreak now gave woods their sight
So flickered through came shafts of light
For nature's silence disappears
As whispers falling from the tears
The tear drops fall from wilted larch
Their drum sounds called the old death march
And from his cradle to his grave the digger's boots end rightful place

With peace there came this mighty price
The storm which turns men into mice
We cannot fight but only bow
To shout and swear from battered brow
Succumb let mother nature's storms
Do there will do their scorn
Then bow in hope that they'll not break
to keep our souls the storms would take.

No Harm See

Glenn Muir

I said “Hello Johnnie, long time no see”
Frae the look oan his face,though, he didnae ken me
I telt him ma name an’shook the man’s hand
At the inn o’ Blackness that stood oan the strand

The penny drapped, his face broke intae a smile
Since oor last meeting he’d been monie a mile
He’d a grip oan ma haun (as if feart tae let go)
“How’s yer mither an’ faither”, he wanted tae know

“Dae they still bide in Lithgie, across frae the wynd”
“It’s weel I remember, they were aywiss sae kind”
Wis it forty years gone? In ma mind I could see
Maw aye gi’ed him a kitkat an’ a hot cup o’tea

Aye on a Setterday, efter the races
He wid come in the door wi’ yin o’his cases
Johnnie’s patter wis braw, ye can tak it frae me
“Bargain for you my friend, no harm see”

I look at him noo, jist a withered auld man
Still oan the road in his wee battered van
Though the hair oan his heid is whiter than snaw
He has the hert o’ a tiger, the bravest of a’

Sad Craw

Davie Cunningham

Ye shaddie- play o Doom itsel — *shadow*
Hertless wi-in yer mirk-bleck shell, — *within, black as night*
O gleamin feathers. Hatched in Hell!
Bad in aw weathers-
Yer kraaw scraichs oot its passin bell — *harshly shrieks*
Fir life's frail tethers.

Thus, when I saw ye stoopin ower
Some baist new-welcomed tae Daith's bower, — *beast/Death*
Fixin yer single-mindit glower
On this nutrition-
Makin it courses Yin tae Fower
Seemed yer ambition.

Yet inconsistencies were noted…
Nae silent rippin but fil-throated
Kraaws rasped frae beak no yet bluid-coated.
Why fetch a flock
O gourmands doon? Ye'd no leave gloated-
They'd munch amok!

Then, drawin close, I saw it aw –
Mair complex than the Primal Law
That, saiconds efter onie faw — *seconds*
Ye're nocht but meat
As riddy tooth, claw, paw an jaw
Seek oot their treat.

Yer angilt neb, yer noddin heid *nose*
Wir no destroyin but insteid
Made new sense o that funeral weed
Yer clan aw wear,
Fir ye wir grievin fir the deid
Yin liggin there. *lyin*

Wis it yer mate, yer bonnie dear
Husband or wife fir monie a year
Nest- biggin chum whae kent yer queer *building*
Auld weys an made
Allooances for each daft fear
And escapade?

Or some boon foragin companion
Ye'd squabble wi ower guts o cairrion
But ay alertit when ye fund an *always*
Ailin yowe lamb *ailing ewe*
Or when a bizzard needit herryin *buzzard, scaring off*
Coorse big broon bam!

I've lately learnt craws arenae lackin
In aw the tricks o problem-crackin…
There's some smert primates micht be chappin
At tasks you've solved.
Magpies cin learn tae curse in Latin –
But you've evolved!

Sae, zingin thro' thon crummock heid, *shepherd's crook*
(Alang wi volts o urgent greed)
Have you got oor self-hermin need
For loss an pain?
Whit soldered that cruel lovin lead
Ontae yer brain?

Craws, keep this unner lock an key
Or else Reality T.V.
Will stick a camera up yer tree.
Ye'll mak yer name,
Trade freedom fir their paltry fee
And end in shame.

I'd no watch. I'm no sentimental
I ken life's teuch and elemental *tough*
Me…you, we've got it oot on rental
An no fir lang.
Yet noo I'll ay hear something gentle
In your snell sang. *sharp/harsh*

Second Time *(For Alex)*

Mary Cuerden

It came quietly not in a rush like the passion of youth
Gently and calmly hardly noticed in truth
It grew from the comforting of deep loss and pain
And slowly it taught me that I could smile again

It started with a treasured friendship at first
Waited patiently until I had got over the worst
It took me from darkness and back into light
Gave me warm summer day not long lonely night

While in my heart there's a place well maintained
Where past precious memories can be retained
Now each morning I thank God that I have found
That love's just as beautiful second time round

Olympics London 2012

Christine McGhie

Did you ever see such a spectacular sight, it had to be the tv highlight of the year
It started with a starring role for the Queen, and a sneak preview of her rear
The spectacular opening ceremony was only the start
So many brave achievements that really lifted your heart
The first four days came and went with no gold medal in sight
But then Helen Glover and Heather Stanning gave the oposition a fright
At Eton Dorney they set the ball rolling with the first olympic gold
And then it was one after another as events began to unfold
The golds totted up with team GB excelling in so many sports
So many simply gave their all, like Andy Murray out on the tennis courts
Braveheart Sir Chris Hoy went storming around the velodrome
Wonderful achievements by our athletes in the country that we all call home
Jonny and Alistair Brownlee gave their all in the Triathlon
How do you find the stamina to swim 1500 metres, cycle 43k and then finish off with a 10,000 metre run
And they even manage to call it fun
It looked more like torture to me and I was just sitting on my settee

Louis Smith looked like he had the strength of an ox
Mo Farrah outran the competition in the 5000 and 10,000
Like an old wily fox
They call him the Mobot, he looked more like a robot
Maybe he runs on Duracell
Who cares, he can certainly run like hell
Team GB excelled in all the equestrian sports
Horses and riders all showing they shared a special rapport
A gold for Nicola Adams, our first female boxer
She certainly gave her opponent a few sore punches on the oxter
Bradley Wiggins looked the king of cool sitting on the winners throne at Hampton Court
Victoria Pendleton waved us a tearful goodbye after being a great ambassador for her sport
Ben Ainslie proved that he, not Britannia ruled the waves
Another gold to add to his tally, and the title he did crave
The performances from Jess Ennis simply stunned us all
Greg Rutherford ran so hard for the long jump, I thought he might end up in the mall
I could go on and on about the most spectacular sporting event that I can ever recall
I would give a Knighthood to them all.

Roses Are Special

Fran Thomson

He gave me a rose the day we first met
The look in his eyes I cannot forget
Hope for the future? How could we know
True love would blossom and quickly grow

He gave me a rose every year after this
On our anniversary, with a soft kiss
No words were needed, unspoken love
Linked us together – a hand in a glove

He gave me a rose as each child was born
All made of silk, scarlet and warm
I kept them together in a large vase
They cheered me up on miserable days

When he took ill my joy disappeared
Doctors confirmed the thing that I feared
He slipped away quietly holding my hand
I was heartbroken, did not understand

I gave him a rose when I said goodbye
Placed it on his coffin still asking why
My soul mate, my darling, taken above
No more silk roses from my true love

Here by my bed these flowers give me pleasure
Some are quite worn but each one I treasure
When my time comes and my eyes finally close
I know he'll be waiting to give me a rose!

Holiday

Derek Cavan

Holiday the wife says, those words sure lit up my face. I said dinnae worry hen I will pack the case, yer erse in a tinny, her reply I received so sharp. She says a man packing my case, wheest man, ha ha dinnae be sae daft! I said, just the thought of a holiday, me and you without our cases, jist at that all the weans came bounding doon the stairs. Where are we going dad, when are we off, is it going to be hot, bubble popped, thought thwarped and me left without a hope. Booked to fly from Edinburgh, Palma bound we surely were. All the clampits at the airport, attracting the usual stare. But us we weren't bothered, a family we were, truly complete, factor 50 was for me, I didn't want burnt feet. The bus from the airport surely was something else, the bairns laughing at other folk, that surely got raw deals! It came to our apartment, a place I know so well. At least I know within 5 minutes walk there was a freezing San Miguel. The biggest embarrassment of the holiday that I truly don't condone, was the maid saying "santa maria" when she caught me on the throne. Many doors have been slammed on me, but that one was so fast, with a horrific face she had on her, a memory sure to last. I must say our family holidays, we always have a blast, and with that gives us memories, ones that are sure to last.

Highland Games

May Ross

Ah was gae'in tae the Highland Games
One Saturday in May.
When ah came upon a stranger
In Bathgate for the day.
He asked why aw' the excitement
An' whits that awfy noise.
I said that's the Haggis for the lunch
Bein' killed by a bunch o' boys.
The sun was shinin' – whit a treat
We had tae shield oor eyes.
The scene aroon'sae colourful
Tinged wi' the smell o' – French Fries.
We paid oor way in tae the field
The grass wis emerald green.
The man' s eyes were like organ stops
As he watched the manic scene.
Pipe Bands playin', cabers tossin'
And, oh, the bonny wee dancers.

Stalls sellin' this and stalls sellin' that
Oh, whit a load o' chancers.
I met him later in the day
In the bar he had been stewin'
For a wee drink here and a wee drink there
It's as weel he wisnae drivin'.
The salute frae the pipes tae the Chieftain
Was an end tae a magical day.
The soond went up through the Bathgate hills
As the crowds a' melted away
But we will ever keep oor Games
And Scotland will keep her culture
Her music, her dance and her customs.
These things we'll always nurture
So here's tae the wonderful Bathgate Games
Said the man as he staggered awa'
So ah'll raise a glass in yer honour he said
And sit doon before ah fa'.

My Only True Love

Kenneth McRae

What is it like to be loved by one woman?
To hold her tightly in your arms
To give to her and her alone your heart
Your affection, your love
To keep her safe, secure in the knowledge
that she was yours and yours alone
Bound together through life and love
She returned that devotion and love

Even death cannot break the love
we had for each other
'Death where is thy sting?'
Not between me and my true love.
My heart aches when I think of her
I miss her, her voice, her smile.
Her memory means more to me
Than this empty life I live.

You were my star, sparkling bright
You were my moon, that lit the light
You were a rose in a garden of weeds
You were a pearl, in a necklace of beads.
You were my mate, my life
You were mine, my wife
Over the years you did not complain
Of your hurt, that hellish pain
You are gone, departed this life
My companion, my anchor, my wife.

For forty five years we were as one
Sharing our tears, our love, our fun
But now that I have lost you
A large part of me, has died too
Though you are gone
I LOVE YOU STILL
My Wife, My Valentine.

Farewell Mum

Mary Cuerden

As I sit by your bed and watch you sleep
I try so hard not to weep
I clasp your work worn wrinkled hand
This takes me to another land
The land of my childhood when I was small
And you were young straight and tall
Dark curls surround your sweet face
Of silver grey there is no trace
I'd take your hand as I do now
It always made me feel safe somehow
And if I were to call out Mum
I knew that you would quickly come
And simply dry away any tears
Then gently banish all my fears
Mentor teacher my best friend
You're the one on who I could depend
And throughout my growing years
You were the foremost of my peers

With gentle words you would advise
You would never criticize
All my life you have been there
Administering your love and care
But over time we have no control
The years have taken a deadly toll
Body now stooped and bent
Your lust for life got up and went
The twinkle that was in your eye
Been replaced by tired sigh
And as I watch you every day
I slowly see you slip away
Soon I must break our tie
Kiss you tenderly say goodbye
My way to let you know
That dear Mum you're free to go
But selfishly I start to pray
Please dear God just not to day

Flying Pyramids

Lorna Johnston

I dreamed a dream
The other night
Of pyramids
Which just took flight.
They flew across
The desert then
Around the world
And back again.
A dream so vivid
Crystal clear
Making nonsense
Of my fears.
These pyramids
They cannot fly
Of course they can't
But I can try.
To see another meaning where
This dream is telling me
'BEWARE'.
Imagination is a gift
Who knows what dreams it cannot lift.
But no more cheese last thing at night
Then pyramids will not take flight.

My Colours

Derek Cavan

I have a problem with colours,
They call me colour blind.
With 20/20 vision,
It's something I can't hide.

You still wouldn't understand,
If given for a day.
Unless you're colour blind like me,
You know where I'm coming fae.

Exclusive club or is it not,
Disability, that's a laugh.
Don't ask me what the colour is,
Or I'll throw you in that white bath!

Before you say that isn't white,
Don't make me say that word.
The grass is green, the sky is blue.
Ignoramus is that a bird?

Weaver of Dreams

Glenn Muir

You are the gardener-the weaver of dreams
You are the sunshine and the rain
It is by your hand the flowers grow
In their fragrant,colourful refrain

Summer lasts forever here
Your presence lends warmth to this place
Within the secret garden's walls
Of winter snow there is no trace

You have made this a pleasant haven
The regiments of flowers are nice
Red carnations,roses and cornflowers blue
And you,with kind words and good advice

A door marked summer opens
Your smile of welcome beams
We will sit and talk in the sunshine
You are the gardener-the weaver of dreams.

This poem was written for Jan Strudwick and formed part of her memorial service at Edinburgh's Canongate Church on May 11th 2013.

Granda's Wallies

Fran Thomson

Noo a really love ma Granda, bit he's getting kinna auld
He's nearly always moaning – it's too warm or it's too cauld
Pits oan jumpers in the summer wi his long johns an a scarf
Christmas day he wore a T shirt - we a' hud a richt guid laugh!
He goes doon tae the pensioners to huv a gem o' whist
Chats up Jean McGrory but swears they've never kissed
Talks aboot the telly, fitba, racing an the like
Then comes oot and starts shoutin, "Somebody's pinched ma bike!"

He's no owned wan for years so we try tae calm him doon
Tell him that we'll go fur a wee walk up the toon
We go intae café bit he's goat this awfy habbit
O' taking oot the wallies then munchin like a rabbit
The ither day a went roon, he wis sittin near tae tears
A though that he wis ill and in crept the auld fears
"Ma teeth ur loast, or stolen" he muttered in despair
A searched the bed, the couch, in the kitchen, doon the chair

"Ye must huv left them somewhere, whaur hae ye a been?"
He jist sat an stared at me wi tears in baith his een
"A took Jean fur a McCallum doon at that new tallies"
A knew then whaur I'd find ma Granda's bloomin wallies
Doon then tae the café, the wumin stood an said,
"I tink your leetle Grandad ees loopy in ze head!"
A felt quite hurt an told her "Dinny you be daft,
Ma Granda isnny loopy – he's jist goin a wee bit saft!"

On The Slopes O' Ben More

Kenneth McRae

The shades o' night were fallin, an the light wis gettin dim
The wild beasts seemed tae listen tae the Yellowhammer's hymn
A broon owl hooted as it watched the day go by
An the stars began tae glitter in the darkenin sky
The mist lay wet upon the bracken
But oor walkin pace we didn't slacken
We leaped ower a burn an stopped in awe
We looked doon horrified, at what we saw
Huddled in the tattered clothes that he wore
A body, lyin by a fence near the foot o' Ben More.

The grass had grown around him, lyin beside the fence
Climbin from where or too, only God knew whence
When we examined him, we could only visualise
What had been the cause o' this poor man's demise
When jumpin ower the fence, a stane had turned his boot
Fallin heavily on his ankle, he couldnae walk anither foot
An even though he cursed an cried at the Hellish pain
His prayers an cries for help, were all in vain
He shouted, but no' a soul heard that lonely mountaineer
A' alone an helpless, he knew his end was near
In pain, he sat huddled an chilled to the core
Deserted an alone, at the foot o' Ben More.

His cries weakened beneath that blackenin sky
He knew all hope was gone, as he lay down tae die
It was the start o' Winter, in that unforgivin land
An on the old hill-walker, Death laid its cold hand
As the evenin darkened there came a heavy fall o' snow
An from the East, a howlin blizzard began tae blow
It covered him an the land around in its icy hoar
An froze to death, that man, near the foot o' Ben More.

Naebody came to claim the body an naebody knew his name
Naebody could even guess the place from whence he came
He'd arrive in the town, give a nod an say."Aye, aye"
Give a sniff at the air, an a hard look at the sky.
"Aye," he'd say, "this is the kind o' day that ah like
it's turned oot a great day for me tae have a hike."
His last words. "See you later," as he walked oot the door
As he took to the slopes, alone, on lofty Ben More

We knew he wis a loner, an preferred to be on his own
There wasn't very much o' him, mostly skin and bone
But he was tough with years o' climbin the craggy hills
An knew more than most aboot a climber's skills
He'd grip his crooked stick an pull tight his anorak
Hitch higher on his shoulder's his old ex-army pack
With a smile an a wave o' his hand, away he would go
Pacin himsel, no walkin fast, just takin it very slow.
He would hike an climb, in sunshine or in rain
The bleak tors, the splendid hills were his, his domain
An as he climbed he'd hear the red stag's mighty roar
As they both roamed the slopes an crags of mighty Ben More.

We'd meet him, summer an winter on the hill
Walkin with great ease an with great skill
When we met, we'd stop an have a blether
About this an that, especially the weather
Noo as I sit here thinkin about that man, maybe
That was the death he wanted, alone an care free
He was now free as the wind with its cauld chill
Free like the beasts an the birds on that hill
I'm sure he loved the freedom, hikin gave him
Away from the rigours o' his life, who knows, maybe grim
But no longer will that old climber roam
His first love, that mountain has taken him home
The ghost o' that hiker haunts the high tor
On the slopes o' the mountain that is called Ben More

Climbers! When you reach the top, lay a stone
At the cairn to an old climber who died all alone
Take heed, when you venture into the unknown
Never, ever ever go out on the hills on yer own
Go in a group of at least three or four
When next you go climbin on lofty Ben More

A Parody of an Aussie poem

Our Dad

May Ross

No longer can we say goodnight
When we are leaving you
No longer can we come to say
"Dad, what are we to do?"

No longer will see you sitting
In your favourite chair
No longer see you touch the flowers
With tender, loving care

No longer will we see you look
Out on the bowling green
No longer will we wonder
Just exactly what you mean

No longer will we have to watch
The struggle to get up
No longer make a pot of tea
Served in your favourite cup

No longer will we have to watch the tears
Which many times you shed
No longer will we stand beside
A cold hospital bed

No longer know the anguish
That you suffered in the past
So we'll remember good times now
For you've found peace at last

So, we will always say goodnight
And know that your not gone
For in our hearts forever more
Your memory lingers on

Ma Brither Jack

Lorna Johnston

Ah' looked oot o' the windie
Tae see whit ah could see
An'doon below there wis a man
Shoutin' up tae me.
'Hey missus dae ye want some bread
tae feed yer man an' bairns'
Ah jist replied'Naw no' the day
ah'm jist no' carin'
'Well missus hoos aboot some cakes
tae sweeten them aw up'
Again ah' said'Naw no' the day'
T'was then he had a cup.
'Hey missus wid ye like some milk
o' human kindness noo'
Twas then ah couldnie stoap masel'
Frae laughin' boot the coos.
'Come oan ye stupit silly man'
Ah said as door flung open
'Ye cannie fool an auld yin yet
No doot ye will be stoapin'
Ye see, it wisnie oany man
Bit Jack, my long loast brither
Ah hidnie seen fur 40 years
The spit o' ma late mither.

Fur when he offered up some milk
He took me through the years
Tae when we milked the coos oan ferm
It awe returned sae clear.
The laughter, fun, it cam' richt back
When coos were runnin' faster
Cos they took fricht when Jack went near
It was a real disaster.
We hid a richt guid blether
Then he promised tae come back
An' that wis the last ah' saw
O' ma big brither Jack.
Ah heard he perished lang ago
His last words mentioned me
'Tell ma sister Jeannie
No tae mourn me when ah' dee.
Jist think ae aw the guid times
We had oan that same farm
An' always remember
We ne'er caused any harm.
Ah picture Jack in heaven
In fields amidst the coos
It's then ah wipe awa a tear
Farewell Jack ah miss you.

The Funeral *(This poem is dedicated to my youngest daughter Julie)*

Mary Cuerden

The cat was very hard to see
As she stalked beneath the tree
Then with a sudden rush
She pounces on the little thrush
It squeaks and flutters between her paws
Before being surrounded by her jaws
Silencing the wee bird's cries
She heads home with her prize

"The cat has caught a bird"

The children scream
So we start working as a team
We chase her up and down the stairs
Round settees and under chairs
Before she drops it on the floor
Then calmly walks back out the door
I know from the way it hangs its head
That the poor wee thing is dead
The children now in floods of tears
You'd think it had been their pet for years
So in an attempt to restore some order
I suggest we bury it in our garden's border
And when their tears are dried at last
The children set about the task
Soon a small box is found
And a hole dug in the ground
From two lolly sticks a cross is framed
And the wee bird quickly named

The children in solemn slow progression
Walk in a quiet reverent procession
The funeral has now begun
Prayers are said and hymns are sung
To mark its resting place with respect
The cross now stands straight and erect
The funeral now comes to an end
With thanks to those who did attend

My daughter then with hands all mucky
Shouts “Hey Mum we called the wee bird LUCKY!”

Trust You Ken

Derek Cavan

A decided to pit pen tae paper yin day,
A'd just had a blether wae ma pal Ken M'Crae.
He said he was intae poetics, and a was intrigued.
He says we haud a meeting ivry two weeks.
In Bathgate toon, wur sure tae be there.
Come along young Derek, dinnae miss the affair.

A said a like poems tae Ken,
And a luv tae write a few.
Ken said, "Well the West Lothian Quill group,
Is just the place fur you."

On Monday night at seven,
With sure like-minded folk.
We surely love oor poems,
And we love to share a joke.
I'm sure your evening Derek,
Just won't be so dour.
Cos true true Scottish poems,
Are the order o the oor.

Hands Of A Craftsman

Glenn Muir

On a warm summer day, long ago
The scent of new mown grass filled the breeze
My work-weary father came through the door
And from life's labours took his ease

Wood stain, like nicotine on calloused fingers
A smile, gentle, child-like lingers
Like sawdust upon the chequered floor
And working boots behind the door

A carpenter was he (like the Nazarene)
So solid, so straight, so tall
Kindly and sublime, he was serene
In blue and dusty overall

His hands, though rough as sharkskin
They were the gentlest of them all
A comfort to a frightened child
From the white coated doctor's call

The Temptations of Food

Fran Thomson

Why do you always tempt me so,
make it so difficult to say no
Giving off smells that go round the heart,
steak pies and gravy, sweet apple tart
I know I'm not fat, I'm just much too small,
I really was meant to be eight feet tall
I envy my sister, the rotten wee ninny,
who eats like a horse and still stays skinny

They tell me that genes decide what shape you'll be,
well, something went wrong when it came to me
When I look at food it goes in through my eyes,
then travels down slowly to rest on my thighs
I wonder if food has a mind that can tell,
who it won't fatten and who it will swell
We've eaten the same in our house for years,
but my family's thin– it brings me to tears

Some things are fatal like passing a chippie,
even the smell can make me more hippie
I could just take the food and slap it to my bum,
bypass the mouth, the gullet, the tum
My dream is to open the fridge and there find
non fattening tarts, cream cakes and the kind
Instead of a lettuce and some mouldy tomatoes,
what would I give for some nice boiled potatoes!

My family always expect me to cook,
but I mustn't taste, just a smell or a look
It's murder to stir all the pots for an hour
then watch them all eat and enjoy – what a shower
I dream of thick soup, fish and chips and the like
as I sit there and pedal the exercise bike
I talk to the vegetables that I must make
and beg them to taste like a big juicy steak

I'll never be thin, it's just not meant to be
and with so many goodies all around me
Supermarkets are torture, restaurants too
my willpower is quickly going right down the loo
I've lost a few pounds but it's taken me ages,
hidden the baking tins, recipe pages
This diet is dreadful, but food - my old friend –
please stop your temptations till it's at an end!

The Courageous Fight

May Ross

She lay there, the girl, with a smile on her face,
Her room was so tidy - not a thing out of place.
She waited, she said, for death's dark, lonely touch,
Though she never would show it - the agony much.

Her skin was transparent, her pulse was so weak,
Her voice was so faint – I could scarce hear her speak.
She was saying a prayer that death would be quick,
She'd suffered enough – let her no more be sick.

I watched her in sadness and I wondered who
Had given her courage to see this thing through.
She was only eighteen with a whole life to live,
A lifetime of living and so much to give.

Her courage, she said, came from him up above
And when she spoke these words her face lit up with love.
She'd find out very soon when she closed her eyes,
For she knew that GOD was all knowing and wise.

Her lovely, young body was wasting away,
She'd tried hiding her pain through each hideous day.
So I sat with her, quietly, while she rested in sleep
Until GOD's angel came and took her in his keep.

The terrible cancer which had given such pain
Would have to go elsewhere, down some other lane.
So we're here today to help with the fight
To banish this killer and put him to flight.

Oh! It's nice to be happy and healthy that's true
But how would you feel if, one day, that was you.
So I'm sure that the girl as she looks from above
Is still smiling and knows with a heart full of love
That you'll all be generous as you give to the fight
To bring some out of darkness to wonderful light.

Tarzan in the Concrete Jungle

Kenneth McRae

Tarzan swung through the street trees,
What to him he could do with ease,
Showin off, he said, "Look at me",
An swung slap bang, into a tree,
The rope slipped from oot his grasp,
He fell too the ground, with a gasp,
Blood ran down from oot his nose,
He also broke a few o' his toes,

As he lay bleedin badly an in pain,
Round the corner came his partner, Jane,
She said. "You're a right fool, so ye are,
Be like everybody else, an buy a car,
Trees, they're nearly a' chopped down,
When they turned yer jungle into a town,
Of big trees they've not left ye enough,
Another thing, ye cannot go about in the buff,
So come on Tarzan mate, be awful good,
Pit trousers on, an cover up yer man-hood",

At her words, Tarzan was terribly hurt,
"Ah suppose ye'll want me to wear a shurt,
Ach! I'm fed up with stayin in rooms,
An breathin in all they deadly fumes
Gimme a place where there's plenty o' trees
Somewhere where the family jewels dinna freeze
Too get out this place ah will wangle,
Back to where, I can let my dingle dangle,
An I'm getting fed up with all this bungle,
See me mate I'm away back to the jungle,

Where I'll not get run down by a car,
Ah just cannot get used to all this tar."

Last time I saw Tarzan, I had to smile,
He was bein eatin by a crocodile,
So ye see, it disn't matter where you bide,
The grass is no' always greener on the other side.

Memories Of Childhood

Lorna Johnston

Childhood memories are the best
In every family who are blessed
Always a welcome guest
To spend time with.
In my mind it feels surreal
To see the images that appeal
to my mood; and now I feel
at one with all.
Through long hot summers we would play
Hide and seek in fields all day
Ducking down, out of the way
Bitten by corn lice.
Sounds of swishing at the light
Always gave me such a fright

When bedtime drew us into night
Out came Jenny Longlegs.
Kill it! Kill it! I would cry
Every second my voice rose high
Ducking under as it flew by
Whack! There! Done!
A regular ritual I endured
From which I never have been cured
One fact of life which is assured
I hate those things; they freak me out.
Memories will never fade
And in our past is when they're made
For future generations played
Again once more.

The Gardener

Mary Cuerden

Tam knew immediately who it was, not just because he recognized the voice but because of the manner and the content of the remark: "Oh they Asters will no grow there Laddie, they need a dry sunny spot." Tam stood up from his kneeling position at the side border in his front garden and turned round, sure enough it was auld Jo, self appointed gardening expert to the Street. "Morning Joe," Tam said.

Joe ignoring this pleasantry ploughed on with his advice. "Right there under the window is where they should be." Tam scratched his head then replied slowly, "Do you think so?" "Most definitely," Joe retorted, somewhat irritated that his superior knowledge should be questioned. "They'll no grow there" and with that he continued to walk down the street, his little brown and white mongrel following at his heels.

Now there was no denying that auld Joe was usually right, after all his was beyond doubt the best garden for miles, his fruit and vegetables and especially his tomatoes were renownd, but that did not stop Tam and many of the other neighbours from being a little bit annoyed by this fact, and like Tam to love Joe to be wrong just once.

A few days later, Wilma, Tam's wife just shook her head in resignation as she watched him place four plastic grow bags in front of the large picture window of their living room which had been a prominent feature of nineteen seventies architecture. She knew there was no point in arguing with Tam. Once he had made up his mind to do something no matter how daft there was just no moving him.

When the grow bags were in position Tam carefully planted the tomato plants he had purchased from the local garden centre that day putting special emphasis on the fact that they were visible from the road outside.

The next morning Tam made sure he was in his front garden when auld Joe passed with his wee dog on his way to collect his daily paper as he did regular as clockwork every day. "Morning Joe!" Tam called as the old man approached. "Nice day again, thought I would do a bit of weeding seeing the weather's fine."

"Aye nay bad," came the reply as auld Joe shuffled up and leant on Tam's garden fence, his eyes taking in everything in the garden as he looked for something to criticize.

Suddenly Joe spotted the grow bags with their lank spindly tomato plants through the living room window. With a look of utter disbelief he could hardly contain himself as he spluttered, "Yer no trying to grow tomatoes in yer living room laddie."

"I thought I would give it a go," Tam replied nonchalantly. Joe quickly responded, "Ach man tomatoes need special care," and he went on to list all the things that had to be done to grow tomatoes successfully such as temperature control, fertilization with a rabbit's tail, the right amount of liquid feed and of course very careful watering. Tam let the old man rattle on and when auld Joe had finished Tam just shook his shoulders and quietly replied, "Ach I canny be bothered with aw that I'll wait and see you never know yer luck."

"It's no doon tay luck, you'll see all right they'll no come to ony thing Laddie," Joe interrupted and with that walked off shaking his head in despair.

As the weeks went by even Tam was surprised how much the tomato plants grew and he got great satisfaction each morning as he watched auld Joe stop and peer intently at the living room window as he passed to collect his newspaper, but in spite of the fact that there was plenty of green growth on the plants there was no sign of any tomatoes. "I dinny see ony flowers on yer tomato plants yet," Joe said with much satisfaction as he caught Tam by surprise one afternoon in his garden. Tam had tried to avoid getting into a conversation with the auld man because he knew that he would do nothing but make sarcastic remarks and he was right. "Withoot them there will be nae tomatoes," Joe continued.

"They flowers are no far away you'll see," Tam had quietly replied.

"Ah dinny think so laddie," Joe giggled.

"We'll see alright," Tam responded.

"Ah we will," Joe replied.

But sure enough a few days later when Joe passed he could hardly believe his eyes when he saw the plants festooned with yellow flowers. "I think I should get a good crop," Tam said smugly that same night in the local pub making sure auld Joe sitting in his usual seat in the corner could hear him.

"Not all the flowers bear fruit Laddie," Joe added quickly. "I would wait and see if I were you," and with that he stormed off much to the amusement of everyone.

Each day as he passed Joe watched the yellow flowers die away only to be replaced by round green fruit. Now it was Joe's turn to try and avoid Tam and his pace became quicker and quicker as he walked to the shop each morning making it harder for his poor auld dog to keep up with him. Thank God I am on holiday tomorrow Joe thought as he narrowly missed Tam one morning who he had glimpsed out of the corner of his eye rushing out the door to try and catch him.

On the first morning after he returned as he walked down the street auld Joe spotted Tam in this garden. He stopped and was about to turn round and go back the way he had come when he heard Tam call, "Nice holiday Joe?"

"Er no bad," Joe replied, all the time cursing the fact that Tam had seen him.

As he drew nearer Joe's worst fears were realised as he saw through the window lots and lots of red tomatoes hanging from the vines. There was nothing he could do but acknowledge this fact.

"See your tomatoes have come on fine," Joe said almost choking on his words.

"Ach aye," Tam replied coolly. "Nothing to it."

"But how do they taste?" Joe replied slightly aggressively.

"I'll get you some to try," Tam quickly answered and hurried in to the house.

Auld Joe watched as Tam reappeared at the window and proceeded to pick some tomatoes from the vines and place them into a bag. On his return he handed the bag to Joe who quickly removed them one at a time, carefully examining each tomato. He then selected one from which he took a large bite. It was sweet and juicy, every bit as good as his, a fact that he could not hide as it showed on his face. "Oh! No bad for a first attempt laddie," he said trying to sound very matter of fact while all the time he could feel his face getting redder and redder with pent up temper and humiliation. So he quickly pushed the bag into his pocket and hurried off down the street. As he did so he grudgingly called over his shoulder, "Nearly as good as mine," then quickly added, "but not quite."

Tam smiled as he walked back into the kitchen where his wife was busily washing the breakfast dishes. He opened the fridge and from the salad drawer he retrieved a bunch of vine tomatoes he had purchased from the supermarket the day before, saying to Wilma, "Add tomatoes on to your shopping list dear." He then entered the living room where he proceeded to secure the tomatoes he had just taken from the fridge onto the wire from which only a few minutes earlier he had removed the ones he had given to auld Joe.

His wife Wilma once again shook her head in frustration and said to herself, "I will never understand men," as she recalled how Tam had spent hours tying buttercups and then green painted ping pong balls onto these poor plants. "Ah it's just as well auld Joe's eye sight is no that good, he should have gone to Spec Savers."

Three Generations

Fran Thomson

Awa oor Jess, ye daft wee ninny
And bile yer heid in that big tinny
Yer goin tae a dance, no a fancy dress ball
And whit yer wearing won't do at all
Yer skirt's too short, yer legs are too long
Ye'd never call that wee skirt a sarong
Ye have earrings stickin oot yer nose
And whit's stuffed up yer jumper Heaven knows

Yer hair's dyed pink, yer nails are green
Yer lips are a colour I've never seen
You've got clumpy boots wi heels like blocks
Like Minnie Moose wi'oot the socks
When I wis a lass I did things proper
No like you ma silly daughter
I dressed real fine tae go oot on a date
And never made a laddie wait

Ma knees were covered and ma face wis clean
Name o' that stuff aboot ma een
A could walk tall and haud up ma heid
Oh! A wis a beauty, yes indeed
Then Granny spoke up with tuppenceworth
Ye were jist as bad and that's the truth
Remember the pointed shoes ye wore?
Ye still have corns that are sometimes sore.

Although the petticoats hid yer knees
The top ye wore wid have made ye sneeze
It barely covered hauf yer chest
Showing everyone how weel ye were blest
And don't go thinking a didnny ken
Aboot the make up ye wore then
Wi yer ponytail and yer Special Brews
I'm surprised ye never made the news

So don't go getting onti the wean
Cast yer mind back and think again
You've had yer day jist as I've had mine
Awa oot Jess and hiv a good time.

Wet Feet

Fran Thomson

A look of fear passed between Chris and Ben. They looked at the floor of the dinghy. Water was seeping through the boards, sloshing gently around their feet. It was cold as it soaked through their trainers. They hadn't imagined this when they left, laughing and joking from the jetty.

They had set off happily on the adventure which they had planned for ages. "We could sail away and play pirates," Ben had told his brother. "If we take sandwiches and juice we can sail around for hours. It will be great."

Last year on holiday their parents had hired a boat. Sailing around Loch Lomond had been wonderful and the boys had loved it. This was different. They were on their own - no Dad to take charge here! Ben was seven and Chris nine but they didn't feel quite so grown up now as they watched the water rise over their ankles.

"What will we do?" asked Ben, panic in his voice "Should we try to swim for it? I can only do two lengths of a pool. Maybe I'll drown!" Chris tried to sound confident when he said, "No, we will stay with the boat. I can bale out with my shoes while you try to row us back."

They spent ages frantically bailing and rowing but they were getting nowhere. The water kept rising and the small boat seemed about to sink.

Suddenly the park keeper shouted,
"Come in boys – your time's up!"

The Tantrum Club

Christine McGhie

I'm gonna join the Tantrum Club
Its healthier than going down the pub
Forget keep calm and carry on
I'm gonna go on and on
I'm gonna rant and rave, be bold and brave
I'm gonna pick up a baseball bat
And batter that beanbag, see take that
I'm gonna pace around and shake my fist
Let it all out if you get my gist
And now i'm knackered and i've stopped seeing red
And even the beanbag looks really dead
Now I've calmed down I've put the bat back on the shelf
And I'm starting to feelmore like my old self
I even want to say sorry to the beanbag
But at least battering a beanbag didn't earn me a tag

Loads of hen pecked husbands go to the Tantrum Club too
It's better than the wives getting knocked black and blue
Hit that punchbag with a snooker cue
No one shouting you punched me I'll sue
Escape from all the wives that nag
No need to reach for another fag
It's just the tonic for anyone that needs it
Stay a while until you have calmed down a bit
Don't keep it bottled up, just let it all go
It's good for the blood pressure you know
Anyway that's why I joined the Tantrum Club
Come along too if you like but you better hurry,
  it's nearly full up.

The Ship in a Boattle

Kenneth McRae

Ah look at ye through the dimple,
Tae get in there wisnae simple,
Who pit ye in there ah'd like tae know?
Wi full sails, riggin, how did ye go?

An when ye were carved oot a bit stick,
How did ye get in there, whit's the trick?
The sea, the hull, the spars, the deck,
How did ye get in through the neck?
Ah look at ye oan yer false sea,
Are ye tryin tae mak a fool o' me?
Here ah am gaspin oan a drink,
It's no' you ah want tae sink,

Mah tongue's hingin oot mah mooth,
Ah need a drink tae quench mah drooth,
Instead o' a boat made wi a pen-knife,
Could ye know hae been the water o' life?
Ah ken! ah'll sell ye for tae get a few quid,
An buy mahsel a boattle o' golden liquid,
When a' the whusky ah hae drunk,
Ah'll no' throw the empty in the junk,

A ship in a boattle ah'll try tae make,
Tae crack the secret ah will under-take
When ah find oot how it's done
Ah'll mak a few no' juist the one,
When ah've made hunners wi their sale
Ah'll buy lot's o' whusky an gallons o' ale
Ah'll sit in a bath up tae mah neck
An drink an drink till ah'm a total wreck.

When below the waves o' life ah hae sunk
As ah'm a hopeless, useless drunk.
An when mah drunken life is through,
Ah could be specimen, in a boattle, juist like you.

Young and Old

May Ross

We're Boghall's congregation
Well, that's what I've been told
It made me think about the difference
Between the young and old.

How the young ones think we're past it
And we're more dead than alive
Well, let them dae what we can do
The auld, auld fashioned jive.

So watch them when they're dancin'
Their feet never leave the flair
And they don't know what they're missin
Dae'in a moon dance as a pair.

Have ye heard their music
It nearly bursts yer ears
If they don't put it doon a bit
They'll be deaf by 30 years.

And when it comes tae fashion
They think they've opened the door
Tae a brand new fad and aw' we say
Is - we've seen it aw' before.

They canae wait tae get a car
Wi' aw' the accessories like
How me! I couldny afford a car
I had tae get by wi' a bike.

Weddin' gifts are Freezers and Cookers
How very lucky they are
We got towels and sheets and such
And blanket – wow – the best by far.

And then they have their bairnies
Their nappies aye a' foulin
They just throw them in the bin
But oors wir Terry Towlin.

And when it comes tae washin'
They've got the washin' machine
We had the scrubbing board and boiler
Then hung oot on the green.

Most of their food comes oot o' packet
Tins and boxes too
They don't know how tae cook a meal
Whit's wrong wi' a nice pot o' stew.

Their gairdins are a wilderness
Ma' heart just fairly bleeds
Tae see God's gift tae mankind
Fair covered ower wi' weeds.

And then the summer holidays
They go to sunny Marbella
See me! The highlight o' my year
Wis a day trip tae Portobello.

But we are too auld fashioned
Aw' we can dae is knit
But we're no that very decrepit
When we're asked tae babysit.
Well for aw' I've said aboot the young
These awfy awfy pains
They've done one good thing for us
They gave us oor grandweans.

Snowtime

Lorna Johnston

Softly falling, snowflakes lyin'
Soon tae cover aw the groond
Fallin' thro' the icy nicht sky
Never making ony soond.
Smaw droplets first, an' then the snaw
Begins tae overshadow aw
The landscape an' beyond the sky
We dae not know the reason why.
It disappears tae nothin'soon
The snow melts very fast
A disappointment tae the bairns
'Aw maw' they shout'it didnie last!'
Bit never mind the nicht is lang
The cloods are thickening fast
An' yes, the snow is back again
An' then the bairns shout oot.
'Aw maw bit will it last'
'Ah dinnie ken' says maw
Bit mac the maist o' whit their is
Enjoy whits lyin' while ye kin
Cos it's always bin ma' dearest wish
Tae mac a snowman in the snow
Tae face the way the wind will blow
An' tac in aw the beauty there
But no' when snow lies oan the stair
So tak your wellies aff afore
Ye venture cross the kitchen floor
Cos if ye don't an angry face
Will come oot frae the kitchen place
An' chase ye till the coos cam' hame
Then you've only goat yerselves tae blame.

William Tell

Kenneth McRae

This is the tale o' William Tell,
In a Swiss town where he did dwell,
Watched by a crowd he had tae show,
That he wis guid, wi a crossbow,
He showed his laddie where tae stand,
An hoped his son wid understand,

"Noo ye've tae stand awfae steady,
Ah'll gei ye nod when ah'm ready,
Ah'm goin tae shoot this aipple off yer heid,
Noo dinna make a move or ye'll be deid."

"That's aw richt for you tae say, dad
But some days ye can be richt bad
At hame ah've seen ye let an arra gaun loose
An ye couldnae mak it hit the side o' the hoose."
Ignorin him, on his heid, Wullie placed an apple,
Gave a cough, he had an awfae dry thrapple,
Wullie took 30 paces awa fae the lad,
"Why am ah daein this, ah must be mad."
The sweat wis runnin doon his face,
"Ah must be a right heid case."

He fitted a dart tae his cross bow,
Pulled it back as far as it wid go,,
If he missed his son wi the arra,,
He'd need tae cairry him hame in a barra,
As he raised the bow tae his shoulder,
The air roond aboot got suddenly colder,
He looked doon along the sight,
"Please God, let me get it right."

His finger tightened, on the trigger,
He felt a lumpin throat gettin bigger,
He pulled the trigger, the bolt flew oot,
Makin a straight line for the fruit,
The bolt flew swiftly through the air,
Maist o' the crowd knelt in prayer,

But the arra flew straight an true,
Headin for, you know who,
It split the apple straight through the middle,
As the wee lad in his troosers, did a piddle,
Faither said, "Dinna worry, don't be sad,
Here's half the aipple, ye've been a brave lad."
Wullie has done it an wis proud
An wis cheered by the crowd.

That's the story, o' William Tell,
If ye dinnae believe it, whit the Hell,
If it's no' true it disnae metter,
See if you can do any better.

Jenny's Cruise

Fran Thomson

The sea was like glass, shimmering in the bright sunlight. The Rock of Gibraltar had just come into view and a few other ships were going to and fro about their business.

Ted looked into Jenny's brown eyes and said "There you are Jenny, I promised you would love the Mediterranean!"

He leaned forward and gently kissed the red lips. She was so beautiful – her long brown hair swept round her face by an invisible breeze.

Ted thought she looked like an angel when she smiled like that.

Later that day as the liner glided south towards the Canary Islands he stood at the stern. The white foamy wash stretched endlessly behind them.

"Do you remember how we planned this trip when we first married? It all seemed possible then but we hadn't counted on the twins arriving quite so soon after the wedding. By the time Jason and Jack came along it was difficult enough paying our way never mind a trip like this. They were happy years though – never a dull moment, eh lass?

We should have done this years ago but there was always something else. Well, we're here now!"

He gazed into her eyes then gently kissed her lips. All the love inside him surfaced like a vice to grip his heart.

Ted was found later by a steward. He was lying smiling with Jenny's photo still clutched tightly in his dead hand.

He had kept his promise to her!

Wee TC

Derek Cavan

There's a wee Glesga cat called TC,
His mammy treats him well.
He's the apple of his mammy's eye,
I'm sure he knows fine well.

When his mammy comes home from work at night,
TC's at the door.
Hiding the mischief he has caused,
While doing his daily chores.

When TC feels like a cat-nap,
And feeling a bit of a grouch.
You know where you will find him –
On the Velcro couch.